A Round of Stories by the Christmas Fire

A Round of Stories by the Christmas Fire

Charles Dickens

with

William Moy Thomas
Elizabeth Gaskell
Edmund Ollier
Reverend James White
Edmund Saul Dixon
Harriet Martineau
Samuel Sidney
Eliza Griffiths

Edited by
Melisa Klimaszewski

ET REMOTISSIMA PROPE

Hesperus Classics

Hesperus Classics
Published by Hesperus Press Limited
4 Rickett Street, London SW6 1RU
www.hesperuspress.com

First published in *Household Words* in 1852
First published by Hesperus Press Limited, 2007

This edition edited by Melisa Klimaszewski
Introduction and notes © Melisa Klimaszewski, 2007
Foreword © D.J. Taylor, 2007

Designed and typeset by Fraser Muggeridge studio
Printed in Jordan by Jordan National Press

ISBN: 1-84391-164-7
ISBN13: 978-1-84391-164-7

CONTENTS

FOREWORD

The social revolutions of the early Victorian era had a dramatic impact on the world of magazine journalism. They could hardly have done otherwise. With their large circulations – according to Edgar Johnson, the first number of *Household Words* notched up sales into six figures – Victorian periodicals were a ready-made conduit into the average middle-class drawing room; in many cases they were the only secular influence that a part of the demographic, only now emerging from generations of book-fearing Nonconformity cared to entertain. The specimen Victorian weekly or monthly was, increasingly, a bourgeois production, cutting its editorial cloth to suit the tastes of a new middle-class consumer base. *Punch*, founded on more or less radical lines in 1841, spent the best part of a decade attuning itself to the sensibilities of its readers before emerging as the symbol of the mid-Victorian home and hearth. Nowhere was this transformation more flagrant, perhaps, than in what might be called the idea of the editor. William Maginn, who conducted *Fraser's Magazine* in the 1830s, had seen himself as a 'lord of misrule', egging his contributors on through the riot of Tory bohemianism in which the magazine specialised. Dickens' superintendence of *Household Words*, a decade and a half later, was at once more staid and more purposeful. Nothing could have been more symbolic of the sober conviviality he brought to the task than the invitations extended to various members of his staff in November 1853 to watch the Duke of Wellington's funeral as it passed the magazine's offices near the Strand.

From an early stage in its ten-year history, *Household Words* existed to promote the Dickensian idea of Christmas. By the mid-1850s its additional Christmas number had evolved into an elaborate work by many hands: *The Wreck of the Golden Mary* (1856), for example, which finds Dickens, Wilkie Collins and others impersonating a gang of shipwrecked mariners trying to keep their spirits up by storytelling. But even in 1852, a bare thirty-three months into the magazine's existence, the vision of the festive season conjured up for its readers is remarkably coherent. Here the members of an extended Victorian family and its retainers – 'poor relation', nurse and even charwoman – sit around the Yuletide hearth as the coals glow hot in the grate and the punchbowl is brought in steaming on the tray, each contributing a tale for the general enjoyment. This being the England of the Crystal Palace Exhibition, and Dickens being Dickens, the scent of uplift hangs in the air. William Moy Thomas' 'Somebody's Story' is a fairy-tale framed endorsement of good behaviour; Mrs Gaskell's 'The Old Nurse's Story' offers a chilly – literally – reminder that the past can't always be brushed aside to suit present arrangements; Harriet Martineau's 'The Deaf Play-mate's Story' ends with an injunction to make the best of things and greet your difficulties head on: 'It is so much better to look things in the face.' But despite the occasional exhortation or awful warning, little of *A Round of Stories by the Christmas Fire* is narrowly didactic. Even at his preachiest or most arch, Dickens' writing is always capable of breaking through the barriers of its moral purpose by virtue of its sheer over-excitement with scene: one of the striking things about *Household Words'* Christmas supplement, even in its infancy, is how successfully this lesson seems to have been handed down to his contributors.

Dickens' own contributions – 'The Poor Relation's Story' and 'The Child's Story' – offer contrasting examples of the way in which he chose to address the mass-circulation readerships of the weekly magazine. 'The Child's Story', seen through the eyes of a traveller who meets a succession of children asking him to 'play', 'love' or 'be busy', soon declares itself as a parable of the Seven Ages of Man, ending with a picture of the family's grandfather sitting contentedly by his fire. 'The Poor Relation's Story', on the other hand, is awash with Dickensian specificity: the unfortunate of the title takes his tea daily at 'Garraway's coffee house' and practises elegant economy at his tailor's by ordering suits made of 'Oxford mixture' which look black but wear better. Even more marked is its fatalism – out walking with his young cousin, the narrator fancies that the boy will 'succeed to his peculiar position' – and the spectacularly bleak imagery contrived on the hoof, so to speak, out of whatever materials lie to hand. Thus, coming down to breakfast one winter morning in his uncle's cheerless house, he stares at the great bay window, 'which the rain had marked in the night as if with the tears of homeless people', one of those great Dickens similes-from-nowhere on a par with Mr Pecksniff in *Martin Chuzzlewit* warming his hands before the fire as if they belonged to someone else.

At least two of Dickens' fellow contributors are capable of giving him a run for his money. Mrs Gaskell's 'The Old Nurse's Story', set in a wind-blown house at the foot of the Cumberland fells, marks an interesting stage in the development of the Victorian ghost story, here still heavily in debt to Perrault's tales of stricken children lured out into the snowdrifts, and without the antiquarian tinge that would begin to colour it by the century's end. Harriet Martineau's 'The Deaf Playmate's Story', alternatively, seems thoroughly up to date: an account of a deaf schoolboy made steadily more embarrassed and distressed by his worsening disability, with a keen psychological edge.

Dickens was an editorial despot at the best of times – even Mrs Gaskell was rarely safe from his blue-pencillings – and the animating spirit of *A Round of Stories by the Christmas Fire* is very much his own. Like several of the festive scenes in the major novels they show him projecting an ideal of child-hood, family life and communal jollity that would always be undermined by some of the realities of his own existence. As we know, Dickens enjoyed chronically strained relations with some of his children, repudiated his wife of twenty-two years with a kind of off-handed cruelty and eventually took up with an actress many years his junior. Simultaneously, the strain of personalised myth-making that infects his books, the sense that this relish for children, party-going and the family hearth really only exists in the abstract, is one of his strengths as a writer, for the air of tension it establishes can never quite be extinguished by the blanket of happy endings and moral suavity. *A Round of Stories by the Christmas Fire* offers a formal version of mid-Victorian life, but beyond the circle of firelight a great many less welcome guests can be seen prowling in the shadows.

– D.J. Taylor, 2007

Most people associate Dickens with Christmas because of his enormously popular *A Christmas Carol*, published in 1843 and retold continuously ever since. Following *A Christmas Carol*, Dickens sustained his involvement with holiday traditions for over twenty years, first with four more Christmas-themed books then with a special annual issue of his periodical, *Household Words* (absorbed into *All the Year Round* in 1859). In these yearly Christmas numbers, Dickens changed the composition method he used for the books he authored individually by inviting other journalists and fiction writers to collaborate with him. One of Dickens' earliest collections of such tales, *A Round of Stories by the Christmas Fire*, is a surprising and entertaining display of the varied thematic and narrative styles of Victorian storytelling. In total, the voices of nine different writers appear in this number, and it marks the beginning of Dickens' use of a frame concept to yoke together the stories by his diverse contributors.

The first two Christmas numbers of *Household Words*, published in 1850 and 1851, contained various ruminations on the subject of Christmas specifically. Most of the pieces in 1850 were about Christmas in various places, from India to 'the Frozen Regions' to 'the Bush' to 'the Navy'. For 1851, the first year in which the Christmas number was published as a completely free-standing issue, most of the stories spoke to the issue of 'What Christmas is', such as Harriet Martineau's 'What Christmas is in Country Places' and R.H. Horne's provokingly titled, 'What Christmas is to a Bunch of People'. Some of Dickens' most noteworthy pieces, such as 'A Christmas Tree' (1850) and 'What Christmas is, as we Grow Older' (1851), specifically lay out his philosophy for the holiday, and the contributions of others for the first two numbers were stories or reflections pertaining to holiday games, songs and traditions. But for *A Round of Stories by the Christmas Fire*, Dickens began to commission and collect stories that had little or nothing to do with Christmas at all. Writing to Reverend James White on 19th October 1852, he explained, '*I don't care about their referring to Christmas at all*; nor do I design to connect them together, otherwise than by their names' (original emphasis). In place of the common theme of Christmas, Dickens began to use a narrative frame to tie his own pieces to those of his contributors.

Indeed, the title of this number itself creates a collective and pleasing shared atmosphere. The image of a Christmas fire evokes not only specific anticipation of the holiday season, but also the more general vision of a warm hearth and domestic togetherness. The telling of stories in a round draws upon rich oral and musical traditions, as one immediately envisions the repetition of the tales. In the context of song, this 'round' of stories also echoes Dickens' division of *A Christmas Carol* into staves. The titles of the individual stories – 'The Host's Story', 'The Guest's Story', and so forth – continue to establish the loose frame. Each contributor is presumably sitting around the same fire, and some of the narrators even address each other. The frame concept, then, despite Dickens' stated lack of a 'design to connect them together', invites readers to draw links between the stories. This technique was so effective in *A Round of Stories by the Christmas Fire* that Dickens did not feel the need to devise a new one the following year. 1853's Christmas number was simply called *Another Round of Stories by the Christmas Fire*. While implying variation of the stories in the first round, the title also promised to continue delivering the successful elements of the previous year's number.

(Dickens would later extend a frame story for one other set of Christmas numbers: *Mrs Lirriper's Lodgings* in 1863 and *Mrs Lirriper's Legacy* in 1864.) This gave readers a reassuring sense of continuation, of a return to something familiar, with the expectation of something new at the same time. And, although Dickens was not concerned about the stories referring to Christmas precisely, he did have a strong sense of what type of story met his criteria for the special issue.

For instance, Dickens felt that Reverend James White's submission of 'The Grandfather's Story' was excellent for *Household Words* but not a perfect match for the Christmas number. He wrote to White on 22nd November 1852:

> You know what the spirit of the Christmas number is. When I suggested the stories being about a highwayman, I got hold of that idea as being an adventurous one, including various kinds of wrong, expressing a state of society no longer existing among us, and pleasant to hear (therefore) from an old man. Now, your highwayman not being a real highwayman after all, the kind of suitable Christmas interest I meant to awaken in the story is not in it. Do you understand?

What was the 'spirit' that Dickens felt should characterise these numbers so strongly? Presumably, it is what he called the '*Carol* philosophy' (according to his close friend and first biographer John Forster). The '*Carol* philosophy' includes the idea that compassion for others should guide people's interactions all year long and the belief that drawing upon memories, even sorrowful ones, will restore proper moral principles. These ideals are articulated most strongly in *A Christmas Carol*, and we see elements of them in Dickens' other works, including 'The Poor Relation's Story' and 'The Child's Story' here. Apparently, Reverend James White either did not understand why his story, which does seem to exhibit traits of the '*Carol* philosophy', was not meeting expectations, or he did not care to demonstrate his understanding with a new tale, as Dickens had requested. White's story about an impoverished man accidentally shooting at a bank employee while stealing money from a gig is indeed the story that was printed in this Christmas number. One gathers that Dickens had a clear sense of the 'spirit' he intended these numbers to provoke, but that he would also allow the visions of others to continue shaping it, sometimes into forms that he did not anticipate.

Elizabeth Gaskell's 'The Old Nurse's Story', which became a celebrated Gothic tale, also caused Dickens anxiety. Dickens revered Gaskell and frequently praised her storytelling talents, but their correspondence regarding this contribution reveals a forceful editor who was insistent that she should alter the conclusion of her tale. In one letter, dated 4th December 1852, Dickens brazenly states, 'I have no doubt, according to every principle of art that is known to me from Shakespeare downwards, that you weaken the terror of the story by making them all see the phantoms at the end.' Despite his invocation of the bard and his continued insistence that she use his superior idea, Gaskell refused to please Dickens by changing the ending. Although his practice was to heavily edit pieces for the regular issues of *Household Words*, Dickens conceded and printed the story as Gaskell wished. This is a particularly significant editorial decision because, as with all of the Christmas numbers, Dickens' was the only authorial name to appear in print. He listed himself as the 'conductor' of the number, gesturing toward the presence of other writers without naming them. While this was consistent with some journalistic practices of the period, it also meant that his original readers did not know exactly which stories were written by Dickens and which were penned by others. In this and many other ways, the Christmas numbers provide some of the most intriguing examples of Dickens' collaborative work.

Four of the other contributors to this number – Eliza Griffiths, Harriet Martineau, Edmund Ollier, and Samuel Sidney – had written for one or both of the previous *Household Words* Christmas numbers. Edmund Dixon and William Moy Thomas were new additions to the growing cadre of authors to whom Dickens turned. Their contributions vary, with Griffiths offering up a long verse piece about interracial romance and slavery while Dixon tells a short ghost story. Thematically, Martineau's gripping tale of a deaf boy discovering then struggling to accept his condition seems to have little in common with Ollier's poem about a greedy merchant setting his host's palace aflame or Thomas' story of a German apprentice seeking his fortune so that he can wed his beloved. But, just as the narrators temporarily bridge class and gender divisions as they hear and tell stories around a single fire, the stories themselves share preoccupations with questions of wealth, justice, hauntings and love. Dickens ends this Christmas number not in his own voice, but with Griffiths' poignantly sentimental poem. Closing with the words 'faith and love', 'The Mother's Story' indeed captures the spirit that, for the next fifteen years, would help to propel Dickens' Christmas numbers to success.

– *Melisa Klimaszewski, 2007*

A Round of Stories
by the Christmas Fire

BEING THE EXTRA CHRISTMAS NUMBER
OF HOUSEHOLD WORDS

CONDUCTED BY CHARLES DICKENS

CONTAINING THE AMOUNT OF
ONE REGULAR NUMBER AND A HALF

CHRISTMAS, 1852

THE POOR RELATION'S STORY
[by Charles Dickens]

He was very reluctant to take precedence of so many respected members of the family, by beginning the round of stories they were to relate as they sat in a goodly circle by the Christmas fire; and he modestly suggested that it would be more correct if 'John our esteemed host' (whose health he begged to drink) would have the kindness to begin. For as to himself, he said, he was so little used to lead the way, that really – But as they all cried out here, that he must begin, and agreed with one voice that he might, could, would, and should begin, he left off rubbing his hands, and took his legs out from under his arm-chair, and did begin.

I have no doubt (said the poor relation) that I shall surprise the assembled members of our family, and particularly John our esteemed host to whom we are so much indebted for the great hospitality with which he has this day entertained us, by the confession I am going to make. But, if you do me the honour to be surprised at anything that falls from a person so unimportant in the family as I am, I can only say that I shall be scrupulously accurate in all I relate.

I am not what I am supposed to be. I am quite another thing. Perhaps before I go further, I had better glance at what I *am* supposed to be.

It is supposed, unless I mistake – the assembled members of our family will correct me if I do, which is very likely (here the poor relation looked mildly about him for contradiction); that I am nobody's enemy but my own. That I never met with any particular success in anything. That I failed in business because I was unbusiness-like and credulous – in not being prepared for the interested designs of my partner. That I failed in love, because I was ridiculously trustful – in thinking it impossible that Christiana could deceive me. That I failed in my expectations from my uncle Chill, on account of not being as sharp as he could have wished in worldly matters. That, through life, I have been rather put upon and disappointed, in a general way. That I am at present a bachelor of between fifty-nine and sixty years of age, living on a limited income in the form of a quarterly allowance, to which I see that John our esteemed host wishes me to make no further allusion.

The supposition as to my present pursuits and habits is to the following effect.

I live in a lodging in the Clapham Road – a very clean back room, in a very respectable house – where I am expected not to be at home in the daytime, unless poorly; and which I usually leave in the morning at nine o'clock, on pretence of going to business. I take my breakfast – my roll and butter, and my half-pint of coffee – at the old established coffee shop near Westminster Bridge; and then I go into the City – I don't know why – and sit in Garraway's Coffee House, and on 'Change,[1] and walk about, and look into a few offices and counting-houses where some of my relations or acquaintance are so good as to tolerate me, and where I stand by the fire if the weather happens to be cold. I get through the day in this way until five o'clock, and then I dine: at a cost, on the average, of one and threepence. Having still a little money to spend on my evening's entertainment, I look into the old-established coffee shop as I go home, and take my cup of tea, and perhaps my bit of toast. So, as the large hand of the clock makes its way round to the morning hour again, I make my way round to the Clapham Road again, and go to bed when I get to my lodging – fire being expensive, and being objected to by the family on account of its giving trouble and making a dirt.

Sometimes, one of my relations or acquaintances is so ob-liging as to ask me to dinner. Those are holiday occasions, and then I generally walk in the Park. I am a solitary man, and seldom walk with anybody. Not that I am avoided because I am shabby; for I am not at all shabby, having always a very good suit of black on (or rather Oxford mixture,[2] which has the appearance of black and wears much better); but I have got into a habit of speaking low, and being rather silent, and my spirits are not high, and I am sensible that I am not an attractive companion.

The only exception to this general rule is the child of my first cousin, Little Frank. I have a particular affection for that child, and he takes very kindly to me. He is a diffident boy by nature; and in a crowd he is soon run over, as I may say, and forgotten. He and I, however, get on exceedingly well. I have a fancy that the poor child will in time succeed to my peculiar position in the family. We talk but little; still, we understand each other. We walk about, hand in hand; and without much speaking he knows what I mean, and I know what he means. When he was very little indeed, I used to take him to the win-dows of the toyshops, and show him the toys inside. It is sur-prising how soon he found out that I would have made him a great many presents if I had been in circumstances to do it.

Little Frank and I go and look at the outside of the Monu-ment[3] – he is very fond of the Monument – and at the Bridges, and at all the sights that are free. On two of my birthdays, we have dined on a-la-mode beef, and gone at half price to the play, and been deeply interested. I was once walking with him in Lombard Street, which we often visit on account of my having mentioned to him that there are great riches there – he is very fond of Lombard Street – when a gentleman said to me as he passed by, 'Sir, your little son has dropped his glove.'

I assure you, if you will excuse my remarking on so trivial a circumstance, this accidental mention of the child as mine, quite touched my heart and brought the foolish tears into my eyes.

When Little Frank is sent to school in the country, I shall be very much at a loss what to do with myself, but I have the intention of walking down there once a month and seeing him on a half holiday. I am told he will then be at play upon the Heath; and if my visits should be objected to, as unsettling the child, I can see him from a distance without his seeing me, and walk back again. His mother comes of a highly genteel family, and rather disapproves, I am aware, of our being too much together. I know that I am not calculated to improve his retiring disposition; but I think he would miss me beyond the feeling of the moment, if we were wholly separated.

When I die in the Clapham Road, I shall not leave much more in this world than I shall take out of it; but, I happen to have a miniature of a bright-faced boy, with a curling head, and an open shirt frill waving down his bosom (my mother had it taken for me, but I can't believe that it was ever like), which will be worth nothing to sell, and which I shall beg may be given to Frank. I have written my dear boy a little letter with it, in which I have told him that I felt very sorry to part from him, though bound to confess that I knew no reason why I should remain here. I have given him some short advice, the best in my power, to take warning of the consequences of being nobody's enemy but his own; and I have endeavoured to comfort him for what I fear he will consider a bereavement, by pointing out to him that I was only a superfluous something to every one but him, and that having by some means failed to find a place in this great assembly, I am better out of it.

Such (said the poor relation, clearing his throat and beginning to speak a little louder) is the general impression about me. Now, it is a remarkable circumstance which forms the aim and purpose of my story, that this is all wrong. This is not my life, and these are not my habits. I do not even live in the Clapham Road. Comparatively speaking, I am very seldom there. I reside, mostly, in a – I am almost ashamed to say the word, it sounds so full of pretension – in a Castle. I do not mean that it is an old baronial habitation, but still it is a building always known to every one by the name of a Castle. In it, I preserve the particulars of my history; they run thus:

It was when I first took John Spatter (who had been my clerk) into partnership, and when I was still a young man of not more than five-and-twenty, residing in the house of my uncle Chill from whom I had considerable expectations, that I ventured to propose to Christiana. I had loved Christiana, a long time. She was very beautiful, and very winning in all respects. I rather mistrusted her widowed mother, who I feared was of a plotting and mercenary turn of mind; but, I thought as well of her as I could, for Christiana's sake. I never had loved any one but Christiana, and she had been all the world, and O far more than all the world, to me, from our childhood!

Christiana accepted me with her mother's consent, and I was rendered very happy indeed. My life at my Uncle Chill's was of a spare dull kind, and my garret chamber was as dull, and bare, and cold, as an upper prison room in some stern northern fortress. But, having Christiana's love, I wanted nothing upon earth. I would not have changed my lot with any human being.

Avarice was, unhappily, my Uncle Chill's master vice. Though he was rich, he pinched, and scraped, and clutched, and lived miserably. As Christiana had no fortune, I was for some time a little fearful of confessing our engagement to him; but, at length I wrote him a letter, saying how it all truly was. I put it into his hand one night, on going to bed.

As I came down stairs next morning, shivering in the cold December air; colder in my uncle's unwarmed house than in the street, where the winter sun did sometimes shine, and which was at all events enlivened by cheerful faces and voices passing along; I carried a heavy heart towards the long, low breakfast room in which my uncle sat. It was a large room with a small fire, and there was a great bay window in it which the rain had marked in the night as if with the tears of houseless people. It stared upon a raw yard, with a cracked stone pavement, and some rusted iron railings half uprooted, whence an ugly out-building that had once been a dissecting room (in the time of the great surgeon who had mortgaged the house to my uncle), stared at it.

We rose so early always, that at that time of the year we breakfasted by candlelight. When I went into the room, my uncle was so contracted by the cold, and so huddled together in his chair behind the one dim candle, that I did not see him until I was close to the table.

As I held out my hand to him, he caught up his stick (being infirm, he always walked about the house with a stick), and made a blow at me, and said, 'You fool!'

'Uncle,' I returned, 'I didn't expect you to be so angry as this.' Nor had I expected it, though he was a hard and angry old man.

'You didn't expect!' said he; 'when did you ever expect? When did you ever calculate, or look forward, you contemptible dog?'

'These are hard words, uncle!'

'Hard words? Feathers, to pelt such an idiot as you with,' said he. 'Here! Betsy Snap! Look at him!'

Betsey Snap was a withered, hard-favoured, yellow old woman – our only domestic – always employed, at this time of the morning, in rubbing my uncle's legs. As my uncle adjured her to look at me, he put his lean grip on the crown of her head, she kneeling beside him, and turned her face towards me. An involuntary thought connecting them both with the Dissecting Room, as it must often have been in the surgeon's time, passed across my mind in the midst of my anxiety.

'Look at the snivelling milksop!' said my uncle. 'Look at the baby! This is the gentleman who, people say, is nobody's enemy but his own. This is the gentleman who can't say no. This is the gentleman who was making such large profits in his business that he must needs take a partner, t'other day. This is the gentleman who is going to marry a wife without a penny, and who falls into the hands of Jezabels[4] who are speculating on my death!'

I knew, now, how great my uncle's rage was; for nothing short of his being almost beside himself would have induced him to utter that concluding word, which he held in such repugnance that it was never spoken or hinted at before him on any account.

'On my death,' he repeated, as if he were defying me by defying his own abhorrence of the word. 'On my death – death – Death! But I'll spoil the speculation. Eat your last under this roof, you feeble wretch, and may it choke you!'

You may suppose that I had not much appetite for the breakfast to which I was bidden in these terms; but, I took my accustomed seat. I saw that I was repudiated henceforth by my uncle; still I could bear that very well, possessing Christiana's heart.

He emptied his basin of bread and milk as usual, only that he took it on his knees with his chair turned away from the table where I sat. When he had done, he carefully snuffed out the candle; and the cold, slate-coloured, miserable day looked in upon us.

'Now, Mr Michael,' said he, 'before we part, I should like to have a word with these ladies in your presence.'

'As you will, sir,' I returned; 'but you deceive yourself, and wrong us, cruelly, if you suppose that there is any feeling at stake in this contract but pure, disinterested, faithful love.'

To this, he only replied, 'You lie!' and not one other word.

We went, through half-thawed snow and half-frozen rain, to the house where Christiana and her mother lived. My uncle knew them very well. They were sitting at their breakfast, and were surprised to see us at that hour.

'Your servant, ma'am,' said my uncle, to the mother. 'You divine the purpose of my visit, I dare say, ma'am. I understand there is a world of pure, disinterested, faithful love cooped up here. I am happy to bring it all it wants, to make it complete. I bring you your son-in-law, ma'am – and you, your husband, miss. The gentleman is a perfect stranger to me, but I wish him joy of his wise bargain.'

He snarled at me as he went out, and I never saw him again.

It is altogether a mistake (continued the poor relation) to suppose that my dear Christiana, over-persuaded and influenced by her mother, married a rich man, the dirt from whose carriage wheels is often, in these changed times, thrown upon me as she rides by. No, no. She married me.

The way we came to be married rather sooner than we intended, was this. I took a frugal lodging and was saving and planning for her sake, when, one day, she spoke to me with great earnestness, and said:

'My dear Michael, I have given you my heart. I have said that I loved you, and I have pledged myself to be your wife. I am as much yours through all changes of good and evil as if we had been married on the day when such words passed between us. I know you well, and know that if we should be separated and our union broken off, your whole life would be shadowed, and all that might, even now, be stronger in your character for the conflict with the world would then be weakened to the shadow of what it is!'

'God help me, Christiana!' said I. 'You speak the truth.'

'Michael!' said she, putting her hand in mine, in all maidenly devotion, 'let us keep apart no longer. It is but for me to say that I can live contented upon such means as you have, and I well know you are happy. I say so from my heart. Strive no more alone; let us strive together. My dear Michael, it is not right that I should keep secret from you what you do not suspect, but what distresses my whole life. My mother: without considering that what you have lost, you have lost for me, and on the assurance of my faith: sets her heart on riches, and urges another suit upon me, to my misery. I cannot bear this, for to bear it is to be untrue to you. I would rather share your struggles than look on. I want no better home than you can give me. I know that you will aspire and labour with a higher courage if I am wholly yours, and let it be so when you will!'

I was blest indeed, that day, and a new world opened to me. We were married in a very little while, and I took my wife to our happy home. That was the beginning of the residence I have spoken of; the Castle we have ever since inhabited together, dates from that time. All our children have been born in it. Our first child – now married – was a little girl, whom we called

Christiana. Her son is so like Little Frank, that I hardly know which is which.

The current impression as to my partner's dealings with me is also quite erroneous. He did not begin to treat me coldly, as a poor simpleton, when my uncle and I so fatally quarrelled; nor did he afterwards gradually possess himself of our business and edge me out. On the contrary, he behaved to me with the utmost good faith and honour.

Matters between us, took this turn: – On the day of my separation from my uncle, and even before the arrival at our counting-house of my trunks (which he sent after me, *not* carriage paid), I went down to our room of business, on our little wharf, overlooking the river; and there I told John Spatter what had happened. John did not say, in reply, that rich old relatives were palpable facts, and that love and sentiment were moonshine and fiction. He addressed me thus:

'Michael,' said John. 'We were at school together, and I generally had the knack of getting on better than you, and making a higher reputation.'

'You had, John,' I returned.

'Although,' said John, 'I borrowed your books, and lost them; borrowed your pocket money, and never repaid it; got you to buy my damaged knives at a higher price than I had given for them new; and to own to the windows that I had broken.'

'All not worth mentioning, John Spatter,' said I, 'but certainly true.'

'When you were first established in this infant business, which promises to thrive so well,' pursued John, 'I came to you, in my search for almost any employment, and you made me your clerk.'

'Still not worth mentioning, my dear John Spatter,' said I; 'still, equally true.'

'And finding that I had a good head for business, and that I was really useful *to* the business, you did not like to retain me in that capacity, and thought it an act of justice soon to make me your partner.'

'Still less worth mentioning than any of those other little circumstances you have recalled, John Spatter,' said I; 'for I was, and am, sensible of your merits and my deficiencies.'

'Now my good friend,' said John, drawing my arm through his, as he had had a habit of doing at school; while two vessels outside the windows of our counting-house – which were shaped like the stern windows of a ship – went lightly down the river with the tide, as John and I might then be sailing away in company, and in trust and confidence, on our voyage of life; 'let there, under these friendly circumstances, be a right understanding between us. You are too easy, Michael. You are nobody's enemy but your own. If I were to give you that damaging character among our connexion, with a shrug, and a shake of the head, and a sigh; and if I were further to abuse the trust you place in me – '

'But you never will abuse it at all, John,' I observed.

'Never!' said he, 'but I am putting a case – I say, and if I were further to abuse that trust by keeping this piece of our common affairs in the dark, and this other piece in the light, and again this other piece in the twilight, and so on, I should strengthen my strength, and weaken your weakness, day by day, until at last I found myself on the high road to fortune, and you left behind on some bare common, a hopeless number of miles out of the way.'

'Exactly so,' said I.

'To prevent this, Michael,' said John Spatter, 'or the remotest chance of this, there must be perfect openness between us. Nothing must be concealed, and we must have but one interest.'

'My dear John Spatter,' I assured him, 'that is precisely what I mean.'

'And when you are too easy,' pursued John, his face glowing with friendship, 'you must allow me to prevent that imperfection in your nature from being taken advantage of, by any one; you must not expect me to humour it – '

'My dear John Spatter,' I interrupted, 'I *don't* expect you to humour it. I want to correct it.'

'And I, too!' said John.

'Exactly so!' cried I. 'We both have the same end in view; and, honourably seeking it, and fully trusting one another, and having but one interest, ours will be a prosperous and happy partnership.'

'I am sure of it!' returned John Spatter. And we shook hands most affectionately.

I took John home to my Castle, and we had a very happy day. Our partnership throve well. My friend and partner supplied what I wanted, as I had foreseen that he would; and by improving both the business and myself, amply acknowledged any little rise in life to which I had helped him.

I am not (said the poor relation, looking at the fire as he slowly rubbed his hands), not very rich, for I never cared to be that; but I have enough, and am above all moderate wants and anxieties. My Castle is not a splendid place, but it is very comfortable, and it has a warm and cheerful air, and is quite a picture of Home.

Our eldest girl, who is very like her mother, married John Spatter's eldest son. Our two families are closely united in other ties of attachment. It is very pleasant of an evening, when we are all assembled together – which frequently happens – and when John and I talk over old times, and the one interest there has always been between us.

I really do not know, in my Castle, what loneliness is. Some of our children or grandchildren are always about it, and the young voices of my descendants are delightful – O, how delightful! – to me to hear. My dearest and most devoted wife, ever faithful, ever loving, ever helpful and sustaining and consoling, is the priceless blessing of my house; from whom all its other blessings spring. We are rather a musical family, and when Christiana sees me, at any time, a little weary or depressed, she steals to the piano and sings a gentle air she used to sing when we were first betrothed. So weak a man am I, that I cannot bear to hear it from any other source. They played it once, at the Theatre, when I was there with Little Frank; and the child said, wondering, 'Cousin Michael, whose hot tears are these that have fallen on my hand!'

Such is my Castle, and such are the real particulars of my life therein preserved. I often take Little Frank home there. He is very welcome to my grandchildren, and they play together. At this time of the year – the Christmas and New Year time – I am seldom out of my Castle. For, the associations of the season seem to hold me there, and the precepts of the season seem to teach me that it is well to be there.

'And the Castle is – ' observed a grave, kind voice among the company.

'Yes. My Castle,' said the poor relation, shaking his head as he still looked at the fire, 'is in the Air. John our esteemed host suggests its situation accurately. My Castle is in the Air! I have done. Will you be so good as to pass the story.'

THE CHILD'S STORY
[by Charles Dickens]

Once upon a time, a good many years ago, there was a traveller, and he set out upon a journey. It was a magic journey, and was to seem very long when he began it, and very short when he got half way through.

He travelled along a rather dark path for some little time, without meeting anything, until at last he came to a beautiful child. So he said to the child 'What do you do here?' And the child said, 'I am always at play. Come and play with me!'

So, he played with that child, the whole day long, and they were very merry. The sky was so blue, the sun was so bright, the water was so sparkling, the leaves were so green, the flowers were so lovely, and they heard such singing birds and saw so many butterflies, that everything was beautiful. This was in fine weather. When it rained, they loved to watch the falling drops, and to smell the fresh scents. When it blew, it was delightful to listen to the wind, and fancy what it said, as it came rushing from its home – where was that, they wondered! – whistling and howling, driving the clouds before it, bending the trees, rumbling in the chimneys, shaking the house, and making the sea roar in fury. But, when it snowed, that was best of all; for, they liked nothing so well as to look up at the white flakes falling fast and thick, like down from the breasts of millions of white birds; and to see how smooth and deep the drift was; and to listen to the hush upon the paths and roads.

They had plenty of the finest toys in the world, and the most astonishing picture books: all about scimitars and slippers and turbans, and dwarfs and giants and genii and fairies, and blue-beards and beanstalks and riches and caverns and forests and Valentines and Orsons: and all new and all true.[5]

But, one day, of a sudden, the traveller lost the child. He called to him over and over again, but got no answer. So, he went upon his road, and went on for a little while without meeting anything, until at last he came to a handsome boy. So, he said to the boy, 'What do you do here?' And the boy said, 'I am always learning. Come and learn with me.'

So he learned with that boy about Jupiter and Juno,[6] and the Greeks and the Romans, and I don't know what, and learned more than I could tell – or he either, for he soon forgot a great deal of it. But, they were not always learning; they had the merriest games that ever were played. They rowed upon the river in summer, and skated on the ice in winter; they were active afoot, and active on horseback; at cricket, and all games at ball; at prisoners' base, hare and hounds,[7] follow my leader, and more sports than I can think of; nobody could beat them. They had holidays too, and Twelfth cakes,[8] and parties where they danced all night till midnight, and real Theatres where they saw palaces of real gold and silver rise out of the real earth, and saw all the wonders of the world at once. As to friends, they had such dear friends and so many of them, that I want the time to reckon them up. They were all young, like the handsome boy, and were never to be strange to one another all their lives through.

Still, one day, in the midst of all these pleasures, the traveller lost the boy as he had lost the child, and, after calling to him in vain, went on upon his journey. So he went on for a little while without seeing anything, until at last he came to a young man. So, he said to the young man, 'What do you do here?' And the young man said, 'I am always in love. Come and love with me.'

So, he went away with that young man, and presently they came to one of the prettiest girls that ever was seen – just like

Fanny in the corner there – and she had eyes like Fanny, and hair like Fanny, and dimples like Fanny's, and she laughed and coloured just as Fanny does while I am talking about her. So, the young man fell in love directly – just as Somebody I won't mention, the first time he came here, did with Fanny. Well! He was teazed sometimes – just as Somebody used to be by Fanny; and they quarrelled sometimes – just as Somebody and Fanny used to quarrel; and they made it up, and sat in the dark, and wrote letters every day, and never were happy asunder, and were always looking out for one another and pretending not to, and were engaged at Christmas time, and sat close to one another by the fire, and were going to be married very soon – all exactly like Somebody I won't mention, and Fanny!

But, the traveller lost them one day, as he had lost the rest of his friends, and, after calling to them to come back, which they never did, went on upon his journey. So, he went on for a little while without seeing anything, until at last he came to a middle-aged gentleman. So, he said to the gentleman, 'What are you doing here?' And his answer was, 'I am always busy. Come and be busy with me!'

So, he began to be very busy with that gentleman, and they went on through the wood together. The whole journey was through a wood, only it had been open and green at first, like a wood in spring; and now began to be thick and dark, like a wood in Summer; some of the little trees that had come out earliest, were even turning brown. The gentleman was not alone, but had a lady of about the same age with him, who was his Wife; and they had children, who were with them too. So, they all went on together through the wood, cutting down the trees, and making a path through the branches and the fallen leaves, and carrying burdens, and working hard.

Sometimes, they came to a long green avenue that opened into deeper woods. Then they would hear a very little distant voice crying, 'Father, father, I am another child! Stop for me!' And presently they would see a very little figure, growing larger as it came along, running to join them. When it came up, they all crowded round it, and kissed and welcomed it; and then they all went on together.

Sometimes, they came to several avenues at once, and then they all stood still, and one of the children said, 'Father, I am going to sea,' and another said, 'Father, I am going to India,' and another, 'Father, I am going to seek my fortune where I can,' and another, 'Father, I am going to Heaven!' So, with many tears at parting, they went, solitary down those avenues, each child upon its way; and the child who went to Heaven, rose into the golden air and vanished.

Whenever these partings happened, the traveller looked at the gentleman, and saw him glance up at the sky above the trees, where the day was beginning to decline, and the sunset to come on. He saw, too, that his hair was turning grey. But, they never could rest long, for they had their journey to perform, and it was necessary for them to be always busy.

At last, there had been so many partings that there were no children left, and only the traveller, the gentleman, and the lady, went upon their way in company. And now the wood was yellow; and now brown; and the leaves, even of the forest trees, began to fall.

So, they came to an avenue that was darker than the rest, and were pressing forward on their journey without looking down it when the lady stopped.

'My husband,' said the lady, 'I am called.'

They listened, and they heard a voice, a long way down the avenue, say, 'Mother, mother!'

It was the voice of the first child who had said, 'I am going to Heaven!' and the father said, 'I pray not yet. The sunset is very near. I pray not yet!'

But, the voice cried 'Mother, mother!' without minding him, though his hair was now quite white, and tears were on his face.

Then, the mother, who was already drawn into the shade of the dark avenue and moving away with her arms still round his neck, kissed him, and said 'My dearest, I am summoned and I go!' And she was gone. And the traveller and he were left alone together.

And they went on and on together, until they came to very near the end of the wood: so near, that they could see the sunset shining red before them through the trees.

Yet, once more, while he broke his way among the branches, the traveller lost his friend. He called and called, but there was no reply, and when he passed out of the wood, and saw the peaceful sun going down upon a wide purple prospect, he came to an old man sitting on a fallen tree. So, he said to the old man, 'What do you do here?' And the old man said with a calm smile, 'I am always remembering. Come and remember with me!'

So, the traveller sat down by the side of that old man, face to face with the serene sunset; and all his friends came softly back and stood around him. The beautiful child, the handsome boy, the young man in love, the father, mother, and children: every one of them was there, and he had lost nothing. So, he loved them all, and was kind and forbearing with them all, and was always pleased to watch them all, and they all honoured and loved him. And I think the traveller must be yourself, dear Grandfather, because this is what you do to us, and what we do to you.

SOMEBODY'S STORY
[by William Moy Thomas]

A whole year of Christmas days have come and passed, since a wealthy tun-maker,[9] named Jacob Elsen, was chosen Syndic of the Corporation of tun-makers, in the town of Stromthal, in Southern Germany. His family name is not to be met with, perhaps, anywhere now. The town itself is gone. The inhabitants once unjustly taxed the Jews who dwelt there, with the murder of some little children, and drove them out; forbidding any Jew to enter their gates again. But the Jews took their quiet revenge; for they built another town, at a distance, and carried all the trade away, so that the new town gradually increased in wealth, while the old town dwindled to nothing.

But, Jacob Elsen had no knowledge of this persecution. In his time, Jews walked about the sombre, winding streets, and traded in the marketplace, and kept shops, and enjoyed with others the privileges of the town.

A river flows through the town, a narrow winding stream, navigable for small craft, and called the 'Klar.'[10] This river, being of very pure sweet water, and moreover very useful for the commerce of the town, the people call their great friend. They believe that it will heal ills of mind and body; and although many afflicted persons have dipped in it, and drunk of the water, without feeling much the better for it, their belief remains the same. They give it feminine names, as if it were a beautiful woman or a goddess. They have innumerable songs and stories about it, which the people know by heart; or did in Jacob Elsen's time – for there were very few books and fewer readers there, in those days. They have a yearly festival, called the 'Klarfluss-day,' when flowers and ribbons are cast into the stream, and float away through the meadows towards the great river.

'Is not the Klar,' said one of their old songs, 'a marvel among rivers? Lo, all other streams are nourished, drop by drop, with dews and rains; but the Klar comes forth, full grown, from the hills.' And this, indeed, was no invention of the poet; for no one knew the source of this river. The Town Council had offered a reward of five hundred gold gulden to any one who could discover it; but all those who had endeavoured to trace it, had come to a place, many leagues above Stromthal, where the stream wound between steep rocks; and, where the current was so strong that neither oar nor sail could prevail against it. Beyond those rocks were the mountains called the Himmelgebirge; and the Klar was supposed to rise in some of those inaccessible regions.

But, though the people of Stromthal honoured their river, they loved their commerce better. Therefore, they made no public walks along its banks; but built their houses, mostly, to the water's brink on both sides. Some, indeed, in the outskirts, had gardens; but, in the centre of the town, the stream caught no shadows, except from warehouses and the overhanging fronts of ancient wooden houses. Jacob Elsen's house was one of these. The sides of the bank before it had been lined with birch stakes, and the foundation was dug so close to the water, that you might open the door of his workshop, and dip a pitcher in the stream.

Jacob Elsen's household consisted of only three persons besides himself; namely, his daughter, Margaret; his apprentice, Carl; and one old servant woman. He had workmen; but they did not sleep in the house. Carl was a youth of eighteen, and, his master's daughter being a little younger, he fell in love with her – as all apprentices did in those days.

Carl's love for Margaret was pure and deep. Jacob knew this; but he said nothing. He had faith in Margaret's prudence.

Whether Margaret loved Carl at this time, none ever knew but herself. He went to church with her on Sundays; and there, while the prayers that were said were sometimes mere meaningless sounds to him, through his thinking of her, and watching her, he could hear her devoutly murmuring the words; or, when the preacher was speaking, he saw her face turned towards him, and felt almost vexed to see that she was listening attentively. She could sit at table with him, and be quite calm, when he felt confused and awkward; at other times she seemed always too busy to think of him. At length, his apprenticeship being completed; the time came for his leaving Elsen's house to travel, as German workmen are bound by their trade laws to do: and he determined to speak boldly to Margaret before he went. What better time could he have found for this, than a summer evening, when Margaret happened to come into the workshop, after his fellow workmen were gone? He called her to the door that opened on the river, to look out at the sunset, and he talked about the river, and the mystery of its source; when it was getting dusk, and he could delay no longer, he told her his secret; and Margaret told him in return her secret; which was, that she loved him too. 'But,' said she, 'I must tell my father this.'

That night, after supper, they told Jacob Elsen what had passed between them. Jacob was a man in the prime of life. He was not avaricious, but he was prudent in all things. 'Let Carl,' he said, 'come back after his *Wanderzeit*[11] is ended, with fifty gold gulden; and then, if you are willing to marry him, I will make him a master tun-maker.' Carl asked no more than this. He did not doubt of being able to bring back that sum, and he knew that the law would not allow him to marry until his apprenticeship was ended. He was anxious to be gone. On the morrow he took his leave of Margaret, – early in the morning, before anything was stirring in the streets. Carl was full of hope, but Margaret wept as they stood upon the threshold. 'Three years,' she said, 'will sometimes work such changes in us that we are not like our former selves.'

'And yet they will only make me love you more,' replied Carl.

'You will meet with fairer women than I, where you are going,' said Margaret, 'and I shall be thinking of you at home, long after you have forgotten me.'

'Now, I am sure you love me, Margaret,' he said, delighted; 'but you must not have doubts of me while I am away. As surely as I love you now, I will come back with the fifty gold gulden, and claim your father's promise.'

Margaret lingered at the door, and Carl looked back many times till he turned an angle of the street. His heart was light enough in spite of their separation, for he had always looked forward to this journey as the means of winning her hand; and every step he took seemed to bring him nearer to his object. 'I must not lose time,' thought he, 'and yet it would be a great thing if I could find the head of our river. My way lies southward: I will try!' On the third day he took a boat at a little village and pulled against the stream; but, in the afternoon, he drew near the rocks, and the current became stronger. He pulled on, however, till the steep grey walls were on each side of him, and looking up he saw only a strip of sky; but at length, with all the strength of his arms, he could only keep the boat where it was. Now and then, with a sudden effort, he advanced a few yards, but he could not maintain the place he had won, and after a while he grew weary, and was obliged to give it up and drift back again. 'So, what has been said about the rocks and the strength of the water is true,' thought he; 'I can testify to that at least.'

Carl wandered for many days before he got employment; and, when he did, it was poorly paid, and scarcely sufficed for his living; so he was obliged to depart again. When half his term was completed he had scarcely saved ten 'gold gulden,' though he had walked hundreds of miles and worked in many cities. One day he set out again, to seek for employment elsewhere. When he had been walking several days, he came to a small town on the bank of a river, whose waters were so bright that they reminded him of the Klar. The town, too, was so like Stromthal that he could almost fancy that he had made a great circuit and come back to his starting place again. But Carl did not want to go home yet. His term was only half expired, and his ten gold gulden (one of which was already nibbled in travelling), would make a poor figure after his boast of returning with fifty. His heart was not so light as when he quitted Margaret at the door of her father's house. He had found the world different from his expectations of it. The harshness of strangers had soured him, and there was no pleasure that day in being reminded of his native town. If he had not been weary he would have turned aside and gone upon his journey without stopping; but it was evening, and he wanted some refreshment.

He walked through straggling streets that reminded him still further of his home, until he came to the marketplace, in the midst of which stood a large white statue of a woman. She held an olive branch in her hand: her head was bare, but folds of drapery enveloped her, from the waist to the feet. 'Whose is this statue?' asked Carl of a bystander. The man answered in a strange dialect, but Carl understood him.

'It is the statue of our river,' he answered.

'What is your river called?'

'The Geber: for it enriches the town, enabling us to trade with many great cities.'

'And why is the head of the woman bare while her feet are hidden?'

'Because we know where the river rises; but, whither it flows none know.'

'Can no one float down with the current and see?'

'It is dangerous to search; the stream grows swifter, running between high rocks, until it rushes into a deep cavern, and is lost.'

'How strange,' thought Carl, 'that this town should be, in so many respects, so like my own!' But a little further on in a narrow street, he found a wooden house with a small tun hanging over the doorway, by way of sign, so like Jacob Elsen's house, that if the words 'Peter Schönfuss, tun-maker to the Duke,' had not been written above the door, he would have thought it magic. Carl knocked here, and a young woman came to the door; here the likeness ended, for Carl saw at a glance that Margaret was a hundred times more beautiful than she.

'I do not know whether my father wants workmen,' said the young woman; 'but if you are a traveller, you can rest, and refresh yourself until he comes in.'

Carl thanked her, and entered. The low-roofed kitchen, so like Elsen's house, did not surprise him; for most rooms were built thus at that time. The girl spread a white cloth, gave him some cold meat and bread, and brought him some water to wash; but, while he was eating she asked him many questions, concerning whence he came, and where he had been. She had never heard of Stromthal, for she knew nothing of the country beyond the 'Himmelgebirge.' When her father came in, Carl saw that he was much older than Jacob Elsen.

'And so you want employment?' said the father.

Carl bowed, standing with his cap in his hand.

'Follow me!' The old man led the way into the workshop – through the door of which, at the bottom, Carl saw the river – and putting the tools into Carl's hand, bade him continue the work of a half-finished tun. Carl handled his tools so skilfully, that the old man knew him at once to be a good workman, and offered him better wages than he had ever got before. Carl remained here until his three years had expired. One day he said to Bertha Schönfuss (his master's daughter), 'My time is up now, Bertha; tomorrow I set out for my home.'

'I will pray for a happy journey for you,' said Bertha; 'and that you may find joy at home.'

'Look you, Bertha,' said Carl; 'I have seventy gold gulden, which I have saved. Without these, I could not have gone home, or married my Margaret, of whom I have told you; and, but for you, I should not have had them. Ought I not to remember you gratefully, while I live?'

'And come back to see us one day?' said Bertha. 'Of course you ought.'

'I surely will,' said Carl, tying his money in the corner of a handkerchief.

'Stay!' cried Bertha. 'There is danger in carrying much money in these parts. The roads are infested with robbers.'

'I will make a box for the money,' said Carl.

'No; put them in the hollow handle of one of your tools. It is natural for a workman to carry tools. No one will think of looking there.'

'No handle would hold them,' replied Carl. 'I will make a hollow mallet, and put them in the body of it.'

'A good thought,' said Bertha.

Carl worked the next day, and made a large mallet, in which he plugged a hole; letting in fifty gold pieces, he retained the remainder of his treasure to expend on his journey, and to buy clothes and other things; for he could afford to be extravagant now. When everything was ready, he hired a boat to travel down the river, a portion of his journey. The old man bade him farewell affectionately, at the landing place of his own workshop; and Carl kissed Bertha, and Bertha bade him take care of his mallet.

The boy who rowed the boat, was the ugliest boy that could possibly be. He was very short in the legs, and very broad in the chest, and he had scarcely any neck; but his face was large and round, and he had two small twinkling eyes. His hair was black and straight; and his arms were long, like the arms of an ape. Carl did not like the look of him when he hired the boat, and was about to choose another from the crowd of boat-men at the landing place, when he thought how unjust it was to refuse to give the boy work on account of his ugliness, and so turned back and hired him.

Carl sat at the stern, and the boy rowed, bending forward until his face nearly touched his feet, and then throwing him-self almost flat upon his back, and taking such pulls with his long arms, that the boat flew onward like a crow. Carl did not rebuke him, for he was too anxious to get home. But the boy grew bolder from his license. He made horrible grimaces when he passed other boats, tempting the rowers to throw things at him. He raised his oars sometimes, and struck at a fish playing on the surface; and, each time, Carl saw the dead fish lying on its back on the top of the water. Carl commanded the horrible boy to row on and be quiet – but he replied in an uncouth dialect which Carl could scarcely understand; and a moment after began his tricks again. Once, Carl saw him, to his astonishment, spring from his seat, and run along the narrow gunwale[12] of the boat; but his naked feet clung to the edge, as if he had been web-footed.

'Sit to your oars, Monkey!' cried Carl, striking him a light blow.

The boy sat down sullenly and rowed on, playing no more tricks that day. Carl sang one of the songs about the 'Klar;' and the boat continued its way – through meadows, where the banks were lined with bulrushes, and often round little islands – till the dusk came down from Heaven. The river surface glimmered with a faint white light. The trees upon the bank grew blacker, and the stars spread westward. Carl watched the fish, making circles on the stream, and let his hand fall over the side to feel the water rippling through his fingers as the boat went on. But growing weary after a while, he wrapped himself in his cloak, and placing his mallet beside him, lay down in the stern, and fell asleep. The town where they were to stop that night, was further off than they had thought it. Carl slept a long time and dreamed. But, in his sleep, he heard a noise close to his head, like a splash in the water, and awoke. He thought, at first, that the boy had fallen in the river; but he saw him standing up, midway, in the boat.

'What is the matter?' said Carl.

'I have dropped your hammer in the stream,' said the boy.

'Wretch!' cried Carl, springing up; 'how was this?'

'Spare me, my master,' said the boy with an ugly grin. 'It flew out of my hand as I tried to strike a flying bat.' Carl was furious. He struck at him several times; but the boy avoided him, slipping under his arm, and running again along the gunwale. Carl became still more furious, and fell upon him once, so violently, that the boat overturned, and they both fell into the river. And now, Carl finding that the boy could not swim, thought no more of his mallet but grasped him, and struck out for the bank. The current was strong, and carried them far down; but they came ashore at last. They could see the lights of the town near at hand, and Carl walked on sullenly, bidding the boy follow him. When they came near the town gate, he turned and found that the boy was gone. He called to him, and turned back a little way, and called again; but he had no answer; and at last he walked on, and saw the boy no more.

Carl could not sleep that night. At daylight, he offered nearly all the money he had retained, for a boat, and set out alone down the river. He thought that his mallet must have floated, in spite of the weight of the gold pieces, and he hoped to overtake it. But though he looked everyway as he went along, and though he rowed on all day without resting, he saw nothing of it. He passed no more islands. The banks became very desolate and lonely. The wind dropped. The water was dark, as if a thunder cloud hung over it. And now the stream ran swifter, winding between rocks like the Klar. The wall on each side became higher and higher, and the boat went on faster and faster, so that he seemed to be sinking into the earth, until he caught sight of the entrance to the cavern, of which the stranger had spoken to him; and at the same moment he espied his mallet floating on a few yards in advance. But the boat began to spin round and round in an eddy, and he felt sick. He saw the mallet float into the cavern; when the boat came to the mouth, he caught at the sides and stopped it. Peering into the darkness, he saw small flashes of light floating in the gloom; he could see nothing else; and there was a great roar and rushing of water. He was obliged to give up the pursuit; but it was not easy to go back against the stream, as the oars would not help him to stem the current. He kept close to the side, however, where the stream was weaker, and urged his way along, by clutching at ledges and sharp corners in the rock. In this way, he moved on slowly all night; and, a little after dawn, got again above the rocks, and went ashore. He was very weak and tired. He flung himself upon the hard ground and slept. When he awoke, he ate a small loaf which he had brought with him, and went on his way.

Carl wandered, for many a day, in those desolate regions, and passed many forests, and crossed rivers, and wore out his shoes, before he found his way back to Stromthal. His heart failed him when he came to the dear old town. He was tempted to go back for another three years, but he could not make up his mind to turn away without seeing Margaret; 'and besides,' thought he, 'Jacob Elsen is a good man. When he hears that I have worked, and earned this money, though I have it no longer, he will give me his daughter.'

He wandered about the streets, a long time and saw many persons whom he knew, but who had forgotten him. At last he turned boldly into the street where Jacob lived, and knocked at his old home. Jacob came to the door himself.

'The "Wanderbursche"[13] is come home,' cried Jacob, embracing him. 'Margaret's heart will be glad.'

Carl followed the tun-maker in silence. He felt as if he had been guilty of some bad action. He scarcely knew how to begin the story of his lost mallet.

'How thin and pale you are!' said Jacob. 'I hope you have led a strict life? But these fine clothes – they hardly suit a young workman. You must have found a treasure.'

'Nay,' replied Carl. 'I have lost all; even the fifty gold gulden that I had earned by the work of my hands.'

The old man's face darkened. Carl's haggard look, his fine apparel, all travel-soiled, and his confusion and silence, awakened his suspicions. When Carl told his story, it seemed so strange and improbable, that he shook his head.

'Carl,' he said, 'you have dwelt in evil cities. Would to Heaven you had died when you first learnt to shave the staves,[14] rather than have lived to be a liar!'

Carl made no answer; he turned away to go out into the street again. On the threshold he met Margaret. He did not speak to her, but passed on, leaving her staring after him in astonishment. All night long, he walked about the streets of the town. He thought of going back to the house of old Peter Schönfuss and his daughter Bertha; but, his pride restrained him. He resolved to go away and seek work again, somewhere at a distance. But his unkindness to Margaret smote him; and he wished to see her again before he went. He lingered in the street after daylight, until he saw her open the door; then he went up to her.

'O Carl!' said Margaret, 'this then is what I have for three long years looked forward to!'

'Listen to me, Margaret dear!' urged Carl.

'I dare not,' said Margaret. 'My father has forbidden me. I can only bid you farewell, and pray that my father may find, one day, he is wrong.'

'I have told him only the truth,' cried Carl; but Margaret went in, and left him there. Carl waited a moment, and then determined to follow her, and entreat her to believe in his innocence before he departed. He lifted the latch and entered the house, passing through the kitchen into the yard; but Margaret was not there. He went into the workshop and found himself alone there; for the workmen had not come yet, and Margaret was the first person up in the house. His misfortunes, and the injustice he had experienced, came into his mind, as if some voice were whispering in his ear: the whole world seemed to be against him. 'I cannot bear this,' he said, 'I must die!'

He unlatched the wooden bar, and threw open the doors, letting the light of day into the dusky shop. It was a clear fresh morning; and the river, brimming with the rains of the day before, flowed on, smooth and flush to the edge. 'Of all my hopes, my patience, my industry, my long sufferings, and my deep love for Margaret, behold the miserable end!' said Carl.

But he stopped suddenly; his eye had caught some object, in between the birch stakes and the bank. 'Strange,' he said, 'it is a mallet, and much like the one I lost! Some of Jacob Elsen's workmen have dropped a mallet here, surely.' But it was larger than an ordinary mallet, and, though it was madness to fancy so, he thought that some supernatural power had brought his mallet there, in time to turn him from his purpose. 'It *is* my mallet!' he cried; for by stooping down he could see the mark of the hole he had plugged. He did not wait to take it up, it being safe for a while where it was: he ran back into the house, and met Jacob Elsen descending the stairs.

'I have found my mallet,' said Carl; 'Where is Margaret?'

The tun-maker looked incredulous. Margaret heard his call, and came downstairs.

'This way!' said Carl, leading them through the shop. 'Look there!' Both Margaret and her father saw it. Carl stooped and picked it up, and, taking the plug out, shook all the gold pieces on the ground. Jacob shook his hand, and begged him to pardon him for his unjust suspicions; and Margaret wept tears of joy. 'It came just in time to save my life,' said Carl. 'Happy days will come with it.'

'But, how did this mallet arrive here?' said Jacob, pondering.

'I guess,' replied Carl, 'I have found the origin of the Klar. The two rivers are, in truth, but one.'

Carl wrote the story of his adventures, and presented it to the Town Council, who employed all the scholars in Stromthal to prove by experiments the identity of the two rivers. When they had done this, there was great rejoicing in the town. On the day when Carl married Margaret, he received the promised reward of five hundred gold gulden; and thenceforth the day on which he found his mallet was set apart for a festival by the inhabitants of all the towns, both on the 'Geber' and the 'Klar.'

THE OLD NURSE'S STORY
[by Elizabeth Gaskell]

You know, my dears, that your mother was an orphan, and an
only child; and I dare say you have heard that your grandfather was a clergyman up in Westmoreland, where I come
from. I was just a girl in the village school, when, one day,
your grandmother came in to ask the mistress if there was
any scholar there who would do for a nursemaid; and mighty
proud I was, I can tell ye, when the mistress called me up,
and spoke to my being a good girl at my needle, and a steady
honest girl, and one whose parents were very respectable,
though they might be poor. I thought I should like nothing
better than to serve the pretty young lady, who was blushing
as deep as I was, as she spoke of the coming baby, and what
I should have to do with it. However, I see you don't care
so much for this part of my story, as for what you think is to
come, so I'll tell you at once I was engaged, and settled at
the parsonage before Miss Rosamond (that was the baby, who
is now your mother) was born. To be sure, I had little enough
to do with her when she came, for she was never out of her
mother's arms, and slept by her all night long; and proud
enough was I sometimes when missis trusted her to me. There
never was such a baby before or since, though you've all of you
been fine enough in your turns; but for sweet winning ways,
you've none of you come up to your mother. She took after her
mother, who was a real lady born; a Miss Furnivall, a grand-
daughter of Lord Furnivall's in Northumberland. I believe
she had neither brother nor sister, and had been brought up in
my lord's family till she had married your grandfather, who
was just a curate, son to a shopkeeper in Carlisle – but a clever
fine gentleman as ever was – and one who was a right-down

hard worker in his parish, which was very wide, and scattered all abroad over the Westmoreland Fells. When your mother, little Miss Rosamond, was about four or five years old, both her parents died in a fortnight – one after the other. Ah! that was a sad time. My pretty young mistress and me was looking for another baby, when my master came home from one of his long rides, wet and tired, and took the fever he died of; and then she never held up her head again, but just lived to see her dead baby, and have it laid on her breast before she sighed away her life. My mistress had asked me, on her deathbed, never to leave Miss Rosamond; but if she had never spoken a word, I would have gone with the little child to the end of the world.

The next thing, and before we had well stilled our sobs, the executors and guardians came to settle the affairs. They were my poor young mistress's own cousin, Lord Furnivall, and Mr Esthwaite, my master's brother, a shopkeeper in Manchester; not so well to do then, as he was afterwards, and with a large family rising about him. Well! I don't know if it were their settling, or because of a letter my mistress wrote on her death-bed to her cousin, my lord; but somehow it was settled that Miss Rosamond and me were to go to Furnivall Manor House, in Northumberland, and my lord spoke as if it had been her mother's wish that she should live with his family, and as if he had no objections, for that one or two more or less could make no difference in so grand a household. So, though that was not the way in which I should have wished the coming of my bright and pretty pet to have been looked at – who was like a sunbeam in any family, be it never so grand – I was well pleased that all the folks in the Dale should stare and admire, when they heard I was going to be young lady's maid at my Lord Furnivall's at Furnivall Manor.

But I made a mistake in thinking we were to go and live where my lord did. It turned out that the family had left Furnivall Manor House fifty years or more. I could not hear that my poor young mistress had ever been there, though she had been brought up in the family; and I was sorry for that, for I should have liked Miss Rosamond's youth to have passed where her mother's had been.

My lord's gentleman, from whom I asked as many questions as I durst, said that the Manor House was at the foot of the Cumberland Fells, and a very grand place; that an old Miss Furnivall, a great-aunt of my lord's, lived there, with only a few servants; but that it was a very healthy place, and my lord had thought that it would suit Miss Rosamond very well for a few years, and that her being there might perhaps amuse his old aunt.

I was bidden by my lord to have Miss Rosamond's things ready by a certain day. He was a stern, proud man, as they say all the Lord Furnivalls were; and he never spoke a word more than was necessary. Folk did say he had loved my young mistress; but that, because she knew that his father would object, she would never listen to him, and married Mr Esthwaite; but I don't know. He never married at any rate. But he never took much notice of Miss Rosamond; which I thought he might have done if he had cared for her dead mother. He sent his gentleman with us to the Manor House, telling him to join him at Newcastle that same evening; so there was no great length of time for him to make us known to all the strangers before he, too, shook us off; and we were left, two lonely young things (I was not eighteen), in the great old Manor House. It seems like yesterday that we drove there. We had left our own dear parsonage very early, and we had both cried as if our hearts would break, though we were travelling in my lord's carriage, which I had thought so much of once. And now it was long past noon on a September day, and we stopped to change horses for the last time at a little smoky town, all full of colliers[15] and miners. Miss Rosamond had fallen asleep, but Mr Henry told me to waken her, that she might see the park and the Manor House as we drove up. I thought it rather a pity; but I did what he bade me, for fear he should complain of me to my lord. We had left all signs of a town or even a village, and were then inside the gates of a large wild park – not like the parks here in the south, but with rocks, and the noise of running water, and gnarled thorn-trees, and old oaks, all white and peeled with age.

The road went up about two miles, and then we saw a great and stately house, with many trees close around it, so close that in some places their branches dragged against the walls when the wind blew; and some hung broken down; for no one seemed to take much charge of the place; – to lop the wood, or to keep the moss-covered carriageway in order. Only in front of the house all was clear. The great oval drive was without a weed; and neither tree nor creeper was allowed to grow over the long many-windowed front; at both sides of which a wing projected, which were each the ends of other side fronts; for the house, although it was so desolate, was even grander than I expected. Behind it rose the Fells, which seemed unenclosed and bare enough; and on the left hand of the house as you stood facing it, was a little old-fashioned flower garden, as I found out afterwards. A door opened out upon it from the west front; it had been scooped out of the thick dark wood for some old Lady Furnivall; but the branches of the great forest trees had grown and over-shadowed it again, and there were very few flowers that would live there at that time.

When we drove up to the great front entrance, and went into the hall I thought we should be lost – it was so large, and vast, and grand. There was a chandelier all of bronze, hung down from the middle of the ceiling; and I had never seen one before, and looked at it all in amaze. Then, at one end of the hall, was a great fireplace, as large as the sides of the houses in my country, with massy andirons and dogs to hold the wood; and by it were heavy old-fashioned sofas. At the opposite end of the hall, to the left as you went in – on the western side – was an organ built into the wall, and so large that it filled up the best part of that end. Beyond it, on the same side, was a door; and opposite, on each side of the fireplace, were also doors leading to the east front; but those I never went through as long as I stayed in the house, so I can't tell you what lay beyond.

The afternoon was closing in, and the hall, which had no fire lighted in it, looked dark and gloomy; but we did not stay there a moment. The old servant who had opened the door for us bowed to Mr Henry, and took us in through the door at the further side of the great organ, and led us through several smaller halls and passages into the west drawing room, where he said that Miss Furnivall was sitting. Poor little Miss Rosamond held very tight to me, as if she were scared and lost in that great place, and, as for myself, I was not much better. The west drawing room was very cheerful looking, with a warm fire in it, and plenty of good comfortable furniture about. Miss Furnivall was an old lady not far from eighty, I should think, but I do not know. She was thin and tall, and had a face as full of fine wrinkles as if they had been drawn all over it with a needle's point. Her eyes were very watchful, to make up, I suppose, for her being so deaf as to be obliged to use a trumpet. Sitting with her, working at the same great piece of tapestry, was Mrs Stark, her maid and companion, and almost as old as she was. She had lived with Miss Furnivall ever since they both were young, and now she seemed more like a friend than a servant; she looked so cold and grey, and stony, as if she had never loved or cared for any one; and I don't suppose she did care for any one, except her mistress; and, owing to the great deafness of the latter, Mrs Stark treated her very much as if she were a child. Mr Henry gave some message from my lord, and then he bowed good-bye to us all, – taking no notice of my sweet little Miss Rosamond's outstretched hand – and left us standing there, being looked at by the two old ladies through their spectacles.

I was right glad when they rung for the old footman who had shown us in at first, and told him to take us to our rooms. So we went out of that great drawing room, and into another sitting room, and out of that, and then up a great flight of stairs, and along a broad gallery – which was something like a library, having books all down one side, and windows and writing tables all down the other – till we came to our rooms, which I was not sorry to hear were just over the kitchens; for I began to think I should be lost in that wilderness of a house. There was an old nursery, that had been used for all the little lords and ladies long ago, with a pleasant fire burning in the grate, and the kettle boiling on the hob, and tea things spread out on the table; and out of that room was the night nursery, with a little crib for Miss Rosamond close to my bed. And old James called up Dorothy, his wife, to bid us welcome; and both he and she were so hospitable and kind, that by and by Miss Rosamond and me felt quite at home; and by the time tea was over, she was sitting on Dorothy's knee, and chattering away as fast as her little tongue could go. I soon found out that Dorothy was from Westmoreland, and that bound her and me together, as it were; and I would never wish to meet with kinder people than were old James and his wife. James had lived pretty nearly all his life in my lord's family, and thought there was no one so grand as they. He even looked down a little on his wife; because, till he had married her, she had never lived in any but a farmer's household. But he was very fond of her, as well he might be. They had one servant under them, to do all the rough work. Agnes they called her; and she and me, and James and Dorothy, with Miss Furnivall and Mrs Stark, made up the family; always remembering my sweet little Miss Rosamond! I used to wonder what they had done before she came, they thought so much of her now. Kitchen and drawing room, it was all the same. The hard, sad Miss Furnivall, and the cold Mrs Stark, looked pleased when she came fluttering in like a bird, playing and pranking hither and thither, with a continual murmur, and pretty prattle of gladness. I am sure, they were sorry many a time when she flitted away into the kitchen, though they were too proud to ask her to stay with them, and were a little surprised at her taste; though, to be sure, as Mrs Stark said, it was not to be wondered at, remembering what stock her father had come of. The great, old rambling house, was a famous place for little Miss Rosamond. She made expeditions all over it, with me at her heels; all, except the east wing, which was never opened, and whither we never thought of going. But in the western and northern part was many a pleasant room; full of things that were curiosities to us, though they might not have been to people who had seen more. The windows were darkened by the sweeping boughs of the trees, and the ivy which had overgrown them: but, in the green gloom, we could manage to see old China jars and carved ivory boxes, and great heavy books, and above all, the old pictures!

Once, I remember, my darling would have Dorothy go with us to tell us who they all were; for they were all portraits of some of my lord's family, though Dorothy could not tell us the names of every one. We had gone through most of the rooms, when we came to the old state drawing room over the hall, and there was a picture of Miss Furnivall; or, as she was called in those days, Miss Grace, for she was the younger sister. Such a beauty she must have been! but with such a set, proud look, and such scorn looking out of her handsome eyes, with her eyebrows just a little raised, as if she wondered how any one could have the impertinence to look at her; and her lip curled at us, as we stood there gazing. She had a dress on, the like of which I had never seen before, but it was all the fashion when she was young; a hat of some soft white stuff like beaver, pulled a little over her brows, and a beautiful plume of feathers sweeping round it on one side; and her gown of blue satin was open in front to a quilted white stomacher.[16]

'Well, to be sure!' said I, when I had gazed my fill. 'Flesh is grass,[17] they do say; but who would have thought that Miss Furnivall had been such an out-and-out beauty, to see her now?'

'Yes,' said Dorothy. 'Folks change sadly. But if what my master's father used to say was true, Miss Furnivall, the elder sister, was handsomer than Miss Grace. Her picture is here somewhere; but, if I show it you, you must never let on, even to James, that you have seen it. Can the little lady hold her tongue, think you?' asked she.

I was not so sure, for she was such a little sweet, bold, open-spoken child, so I set her to hide herself; and then I helped Dorothy to turn a great picture, that leaned with its face towards the wall, and was not hung up as the others were. To be sure, it beat Miss Grace for beauty; and, I think, for scornful

44

pride, too, though in that matter it might be hard to choose. I could have looked at it an hour, but Dorothy seemed half frightened of having shown it to me, and hurried it back again, and bade me run and find Miss Rosamond, for that there were some ugly places about the house, where she should like ill for the child to go. I was a brave, high-spirited girl, and thought little of what the old woman said, for I liked hide-and-seek as well as any child in the parish; so off I ran to find my little one.

As winter drew on, and the days grew shorter, I was sometimes almost certain that I heard a noise as if someone was playing on the great organ in the hall. I did not hear it every evening; but, certainly, I did very often; usually when I was sitting with Miss Rosamond, after I had put her to bed, and keeping quite still and silent in the bedroom. Then I used to hear it booming and swelling away in the distance. The first night, when I went down to my supper, I asked Dorothy who had been playing music, and James said very shortly that I was a gowk[18] to take the wind soughing among the trees for music; but I saw Dorothy look at him very fearfully, and Bessy,[19] the kitchenmaid, said something beneath her breath, and went quite white. I saw they did not like my question, so I held my peace till I was with Dorothy alone, when I knew I could get a good deal out of her. So, the next day, I watched my time, and I coaxed and asked her who it was that played the organ; for I knew that it was the organ and not the wind well enough, for all I had kept silence before James. But Dorothy had had her lesson, I'll warrant, and never a word could I get from her. So then I tried Bessy, though I had always held my head rather above her, as I was evened to James and Dorothy, and she was little better than their servant. So she said I must never, never tell; and, if I ever told, I was never to say *she* had told me; but it was a very strange noise, and she had heard it many a time, but most of all on winter nights, and before storms; and folks did say, it was the old lord playing on the great organ in the hall, just as he used to do when he was alive; but who the old lord was, or why he played, and why he played on stormy winter evenings in particular, she either could not or would not tell me. Well! I told you I had a brave heart; and I thought it was rather pleasant to have that grand music rolling about the house, let who would be the player; for now it rose above the great gusts of wind, and wailed and triumphed just like a living creature, and then it fell to a softness most complete; only it was always music and tunes, so it was nonsense to call it the wind. I thought, at first, it might be Miss Furnivall who played, unknown to Bessy; but, one day when I was in the hall by myself, I opened the organ and peeped all about it, and around it, as I had done to the organ in Crosthwaite Church once before, and I saw it was all broken and destroyed inside, though it looked so brave and fine; and then, though it was noon-day, my flesh began to creep a little, and I shut it up, and ran away pretty quickly to my own bright nursery; and I did not like hearing the music for some time after that, any more than James and Dorothy did. All this time Miss Rosamond was making herself more and more beloved. The old ladies liked her to dine with them at their early dinner; James stood behind Miss Furnivall's chair, and I behind Miss Rosamond's, all in state; and, after dinner, she would play about in a corner of the great drawing room, as still as any mouse, while Miss Furnivall slept, and I had my dinner in the kitchen. But she was glad enough to come to me in the nursery afterwards; for, as she said, Miss Furnivall was so sad, and Mrs Stark so dull; but she and I were merry enough; and, by and by, I got not to care for that weird rolling music, which did one no harm, if we did not know where it came from.

That winter was very cold. In the middle of October the frosts began, and lasted many, many weeks. I remember, one day at dinner, Miss Furnivall lifted up her sad, heavy eyes, and said to Mrs Stark, 'I am afraid we shall have a terrible winter,' in a strange kind of meaning way. But Mrs Stark pretended not to hear, and talked very loud of something else. My little lady and I did not care for the frost; – not we! As long as it was dry we climbed up the steep brows, behind the house, and went up on the Fells, which were bleak and bare enough, and there we ran races in the fresh, sharp air; and once we came down by a new path that took us past the two old gnarled holly trees, which grew about halfway down by the east side of the house. But the days grew shorter and shorter; and the old lord, if it was he, played away more and more stormily and sadly on the great organ. One Sunday afternoon, – it must have been towards the end of November – I asked Dorothy to take charge of little Missey when she came out of the drawing room, after Miss Furnivall had had her nap; for it was too cold to take her with me to church, and yet I wanted to go. And Dorothy was glad enough to promise, and was so fond of the child that all seemed well; and Bessy and I set off very briskly, though the sky hung heavy and black over the white earth, as if the night had never fully gone away; and the air, though still, was very biting and keen.

'We shall have a fall of snow,' said Bessy to me. And sure enough, even while we were in church, it came down thick, in great large flakes, so thick it almost darkened the windows. It had stopped snowing before we came out, but it lay soft, thick and deep beneath our feet, as we tramped home. Before we got to the hall the moon rose, and I think it was lighter then, – what with the moon, and what with the white dazzling snow – than it had been when we went to church, between two and three o'clock. I have not told you that Miss Furnivall and Mrs Stark never went to church: they used to read the prayers together, in their quiet gloomy way; they seemed to feel the Sunday very long without their tapestry work to be busy at. So when I went to Dorothy in the kitchen, to fetch Miss Rosamond and take her upstairs with me, I did not much wonder when the old woman told me that the ladies had kept the child with them, and that she had never come to the kitchen, as I had bidden her, when she was tired of behaving pretty in the drawing room. So I took off my things and went to find her, and bring her to her supper in the nursery. But when I went into the best drawing room, there sat the two old ladies, very still and quiet, dropping out a word now and then, but looking as if nothing so bright and merry as Miss Rosamond had ever been near them. Still I thought she might be hiding from me; it was one of her pretty ways; and that she had persuaded them to look as if they knew nothing about her; so I went softly peeping under this sofa, and behind that chair, making believe I was sadly frightened at not finding her.

'What's the matter, Hester?' said Mrs Stark sharply. I don't know if Miss Furnivall had seen me, for, as I told you, she was very deaf, and she sat quite still, idly staring into the fire, with her hopeless face. 'I'm only looking for my little Rosy-Posy,' replied I, still thinking that the child was there, and near me, though I could not see her.

'Miss Rosamond is not here,' said Mrs Stark. 'She went away more than an hour ago to find Dorothy.' And she too turned and went on looking into the fire.

My heart sank at this, and I began to wish I had never left my darling. I went back to Dorothy and told her. James was gone out for the day, but she and me and Bessy took lights, and went up into the nursery first and then we roamed over the great large house, calling and entreating Miss Rosamond to come out of her hiding place, and not frighten us to death in that way. But there was no answer; no sound.

'Oh!' said I at last, 'Can she have got into the east wing and hidden there?'

But Dorothy said it was not possible, for that she herself had never been in there; that the doors were always locked, and my lord's steward had the keys, she believed; at any rate, neither she nor James had ever seen them; so, I said I would go back and see if, after all, she was not hidden in the drawing room, unknown to the old ladies; and if I found her there, I said, I would whip her well for the fright she had given me; but I never meant to do it. Well, I went back to the west drawing room, and I told Mrs Stark we could not find her anywhere, and asked for leave to look all about the furniture there, for I thought now, that she might have fallen asleep in some warm hidden corner; but no! we looked, Miss Furnivall got up and looked, trembling all over, and she was nowhere there; then we set off again, every one in the house, and looked in all the places we had searched before, but we could not find her. Miss Furnivall shivered and shook so much, that Mrs Stark took her back into the warm drawing room; but not before they had made me promise to bring her to them when she was found. Well-a-day! I began to think she never would be found, when I bethought me to look out into the great front court, all covered with snow. I was upstairs when I looked out; but, it was such clear moonlight, I could see quite plain two little footprints, which might be traced from the hall door, and round the corner of the east wing. I don't know how I got down, but I tugged open the great, stiff hall door; and, throwing the skirt of my gown over my head for a cloak, I ran out. I turned the east corner, and there a black shadow fell on the snow; but when I came again into the moonlight, there were the little footmarks going up – up to the Fells. It was bitter cold; so cold that the air almost took the skin off my face as I ran, but I ran on, crying to think how my poor little darling must be perished and frightened. I was within sight of the holly trees, when I saw a shepherd coming down the hill, bearing something in his arms wrapped in his maud.[20] He shouted to me, and asked me if I had lost a bairn; and, when I could not speak for crying, he bore towards me, and I saw my wee bairnie lying still, and white, and stiff, in his arms, as if she had been dead. He told me he had been up the Fells to gather in his sheep, before the deep cold of night came on, and that under the holly trees (black marks on the hillside, where no other bush was for miles around) he had found my little lady – my lamb – my queen – my darling – stiff and cold, in the terrible sleep which is frost-begotten. Oh! the joy, and the tears of having her in my arms once again! for I would not let him carry her; but took her, maud and all, into my own arms, and held her near my own warm neck and heart, and felt the life stealing slowly back again into her little gentle limbs. But she was still insensible when we reached the hall, and I had no breath for speech. We went in by the kitchen door.

'Bring the warming pan,' said I; and I carried her upstairs and began undressing her by the nursery fire, which Bessy had kept up. I called my little lammie all the sweet and playful names I could think of, – even while my eyes were blinded by my tears; and at last, oh! at length she opened her large blue eyes. Then I put her into her warm bed, and sent Dorothy down to tell Miss Furnivall that all was well; and I made up my mind to sit by my darling's bedside the live-long night. She fell away into a soft sleep as soon as her pretty head had touched the pillow, and I watched by her till morning light; when she wakened up bright and clear – or so I thought at first – and, my dears, so I think now.

She said, that she had fancied that she should like to go to Dorothy, for that both the old ladies were asleep, and it was very dull in the drawing room; and that, as she was going through the west lobby, she saw the snow through the high window falling – falling – soft and steady; but she wanted to see it lying pretty and white on the ground; so she made her way into the great hall; and then, going to the window, she saw it bright and soft upon the drive; but while she stood there, she saw a little girl, not so old as she was, 'but so pretty,' said my darling, 'and this little girl beckoned to me to come out; and oh, she was so pretty and so sweet, I could not choose but go.' And then this other little girl had taken her by the hand, and side by side the two had gone round the east corner.

'Now you are a naughty little girl, and telling stories,' said I. 'What would your good mamma, that is in heaven, and never told a story in her life, say to her little Rosamond, if she heard her – and I dare say she does – telling stories!'

'Indeed, Hester,' sobbed out my child; 'I'm telling you true. Indeed I am.'

'Don't tell me!' said I, very stern. 'I tracked you by your footmarks through the snow; there were only yours to be seen: and if you had had a little girl to go hand-in-hand with you up the hill, don't you think the footprints would have gone along with yours?'

'I can't help it, dear, dear Hester,' said she, crying, 'if they did not; I never looked at her feet, but she held my hand fast and tight in her little one, and it was very, very cold. She took me up the Fell path, up to the holly trees; and there I saw a lady weeping and crying; but when she saw me, she hushed her weeping, and smiled very proud and grand, and took me

51

on her knee, and began to lull me to sleep; and that's all, Hester – but that is true; and my dear mamma knows it is,' said she, crying. So I thought the child was in a fever, and pretended to believe her, as she went over her story – over and over again, and always the same. At last Dorothy knocked at the door with Miss Rosamond's breakfast; and she told me the old ladies were down in the eating parlour, and that they wanted to speak to me. They had both been into the night nursery the evening before, but it was after Miss Rosamond was asleep; so they had only looked at her – not asked me any questions.

'I shall catch it,' thought I to myself, as I went along the north gallery. 'And yet,' I thought, taking courage, 'it was in their charge I left her; and it's they that's to blame for letting her steal away unknown and unwatched.' So I went in boldly, and told my story. I told it all to Miss Furnivall, shouting it close to her ear; but when I came to the mention of the other little girl out in the snow, coaxing and tempting her out, and wiling her up to the grand and beautiful lady by the holly tree, she threw her arms up – her old and withered arms – and cried aloud, 'Oh! Heaven, forgive! Have mercy!'

Mrs Stark took hold of her; roughly enough, I thought; but she was past Mrs Stark's management, and spoke to me, in a kind of wild warning and authority.

'Hester! keep her from that child! It will lure her to her death! That evil child! Tell her it is a wicked, naughty child.' Then, Mrs Stark hurried me out of the room; where, indeed, I was glad enough to go; but Miss Furnivall kept shrieking out, 'Oh! have mercy! Wilt Thou never forgive! It is many a long year ago – '

I was very uneasy in my mind after that. I durst never leave Miss Rosamond, night or day, for fear lest she might slip off again, after some fancy or other; and all the more, because I thought I could make out that Miss Furnivall was crazy, from their odd ways about her; and I was afraid lest something of the same kind (which might be in the family, you know) hung over my darling. And the great frost never ceased all this time; and, whenever it was a more stormy night than usual, between the gusts, and through the wind, we heard the old lord playing on the great organ. But, old lord, or not, wherever Miss Rosamond went, there I followed; for my love for her, pretty, helpless orphan, was stronger than my fear for the grand and terrible sound. Besides, it rested with me to keep her cheerful and merry, as beseemed her age. So we played together, and wandered together, here and there, and everywhere; for I never dared to lose sight of her again in that large and rambling house. And so it happened, that one afternoon, not long before Christmas day, we were playing together on the billiard table in the great hall (not that we knew the right way of playing, but she liked to roll the smooth ivory balls with her pretty hands, and I liked to do whatever she did); and, by and by, without our noticing it, it grew dusk indoors, though it was still light in the open air, and I was thinking of taking her back into the nursery, when, all of a sudden, she cried out:

'Look, Hester! look! there is my poor little girl out in the snow!'

I turned towards the long narrow windows, and there, sure enough, I saw a little girl, less than my Miss Rosamond – dressed all unfit to be out of doors such a bitter night – crying, and beating against the windowpanes, as if she wanted to be let in. She seemed to sob and wail, till Miss Rosamond could bear it no longer, and was flying to the door to open it, when, all of a sudden, and close upon us, the great organ pealed out so loud and thundering, it fairly made me tremble; and all the more, when I remembered me that, even in the stillness of that dead-cold weather, I had heard no sound of little battering hands upon the window glass, although the Phantom Child had seemed to put forth all its force; and, although I had seen it wail and cry, no faintest touch of sound had fallen upon my ears. Whether I remembered all this at the very moment, I do not know; the great organ sound had so stunned me into terror; but this I know, I caught up Miss Rosamond before she got the hall door opened, and clutched her, and carried her away, kicking and screaming, into the large bright kitchen, where Dorothy and Agnes were busy with their mince pies.

'What is the matter with my sweet one?' cried Dorothy, as I bore in Miss Rosamond, who was sobbing as if her heart would break.

'She won't let me open the door for my little girl to come in; and she'll die if she is out on the Fells all night. Cruel, naughty Hester,' she said, slapping me; but she might have struck harder, for I had seen a look of ghastly terror on Dorothy's face, which made my very blood run cold.

'Shut the back kitchen door fast, and bolt it well,' said she to Agnes. She said no more; she gave me raisins and almonds to quiet Miss Rosamond: but she sobbed about the little girl in the snow, and would not touch any of the good things. I was thankful when she cried herself to sleep in bed. Then I stole down to the kitchen, and told Dorothy I had made up my mind. I would carry my darling back to my father's house in Applethwaite; where, if we lived humbly, we lived at peace. I said I had been frightened enough with the old lord's organ playing; but now, that I had seen for myself this little moaning child, all decked out as no child in the neighbourhood could be, beating and battering to get in, yet always without any sound or noise – with the dark wound on its right shoulder;

and that Miss Rosamond had known it again for the phantom that had nearly lured her to her death (which Dorothy knew was true); I would stand it no longer.

I saw Dorothy change colour once or twice. When I had done, she told me she did not think I could take Miss Rosamond with me, for that she was my lord's ward, and I had no right over her; and she asked me, would I leave the child that I was so fond of, just for sounds and sights that could do me no harm; and that they had all had to get used to in their turns? I was all in a hot, trembling passion; and I said it was very well for her to talk, that knew what these sights and noises betokened, and that had, perhaps, had something to do with the Spectre-child while it was alive. And I taunted her so, that she told me all she knew, at last; and then I wished I had never been told, for it only made me more afraid than ever.

She said she had heard the tale from old neighbours, that were alive when she was first married; when folks used to come to the hall sometimes, before it had got such a bad name on the countryside: it might not be true, or it might, what she had been told.

The old lord was Miss Furnivall's father – Miss Grace, as Dorothy called her, for Miss Maude was the elder, and Miss Furnivall by rights. The old lord was eaten up with pride. Such a proud man was never seen or heard of; and his daughters were like him. No one was good enough to wed them, although they had choice enough; for they were the great beauties of their day, as I had seen by their portraits, where they hung in the state drawing room. But, as the old saying is, 'Pride will have a fall;'[21] and these two haughty beauties fell in love with the same man, and he no better than a foreign musician, whom their father had down from London to play music with him at the Manor House. For, above all things, next to this pride, the old lord loved music. He could play on nearly every instrument that ever was heard of; and it was a strange thing it did not soften him; but he was a fierce dour old man, and had broken his poor wife's heart with his cruelty, they said. He was mad after music, and would pay any money for it. So he got this foreigner to come; who made such beautiful music, that they said the very birds on the trees stopped their singing to listen. And, by degrees, this foreign gentleman got such a hold over the old lord, that nothing would serve him but that he must come every year; and it was he that had the great organ brought from Holland and built up in the hall, where it stood now. He taught the old lord to play on it; but many and many a time, when Lord Furnivall was thinking of nothing but his fine organ, and his finer music, the dark foreigner was walking abroad in the woods with one of the young ladies; now Miss Maude, and then Miss Grace.

Miss Maude won the day and carried off the prize, such as it was; and he and she were married, all unknown to any one; and before he made his next yearly visit, she had been confined of a little girl at a farmhouse on the Moors, while her father and Miss Grace thought she was away at Doncaster Races. But though she was a wife and a mother, she was not a bit softened, but as haughty and as passionate as ever; and perhaps more so, for she was jealous of Miss Grace, to whom her foreign husband paid a deal of court – by way of blinding her – as he told his wife. But Miss Grace triumphed over Miss Maude, and Miss Maude grew fiercer and fiercer, both with her husband and with her sister; and the former – who could easily shake off what was disagreeable, and hide himself in foreign countries – went away a month before his usual time that summer, and half threatened that he would never come back again. Meanwhile, the little girl was left at the farmhouse, and her mother used to have her horse saddled and gallop wildly over the hills to see her once every week, at the very least – for where she loved, she loved; and where she hated, she hated. And the old lord went on playing – playing on his organ; and the servants thought the sweet music he made had soothed down his awful temper, of which (Dorothy said) some terrible tales could be told. He grew infirm too, and had to walk with a crutch; and his son – that was the present Lord Furnivall's father – was with the army in America, and the other son at sea; so Miss Maude had it pretty much her own way, and she and Miss Grace grew colder and bitterer to each other every day; till at last they hardly ever spoke, except when the old lord was by. The foreign musician came again the next summer, but it was for the last time; for they led him such a life with their jealousy and their passions, that he grew weary, and went away, and never was heard of again. And Miss Maude, who had always meant to have her marriage acknowledged when her father should be dead, was left now a deserted wife – whom nobody knew to have been married – with a child that she dared not own, although she loved it to distraction; living with a father whom she feared, and a sister whom she hated. When the next summer passed over and the dark foreigner never came, both Miss Maude and Miss Grace grew gloomy and sad; they had a haggard look about them, though they looked handsome as ever. But by and by Miss Maude brightened; for her father grew more and more infirm, and more than ever carried away by his music; and she and Miss Grace lived almost entirely apart, having separate rooms, the one on the west side – Miss Maude on the east – those very rooms which were now shut up. So she thought she might have her little girl with her, and no one need ever know except those who dared not speak about it, and were bound to believe that it was, as she said, a cottager's child she had taken a fancy to. All this, Dorothy said, was pretty well known; but what came afterwards no one knew, except Miss Grace, and Mrs Stark, who was even then her maid, and much more of a friend to her than ever her sister had been. But the servants supposed, from words that were dropped, that Miss Maude had triumphed over Miss Grace, and told her that all the time the dark foreigner had been mocking her with pretended love – he was her own husband; the colour left Miss Grace's cheek and lips that very day for ever, and she was heard to say many a time that sooner or later she would have her revenge; and Mrs Stark was for ever spying about the east rooms.

One fearful night, just after the New Year had come in, when the snow was lying thick and deep, and the flakes were still falling – fast enough to blind any one who might be out and abroad – there was a great and violent noise heard, and the old lord's voice above all, cursing and swearing awfully, – and the cries of a little child, – and the proud defiance of a fierce woman, – and the sound of a blow, – and a dead stillness, – and moans and wailings dying away on the hillside! Then the old lord summoned all his servants, and told them, with terrible oaths, and words more terrible, that his daughter had disgraced herself, and that he had turned her out of doors, – her, and her child, – and that if ever they gave her help, – or food – or shelter, – he prayed that they might never enter Heaven. And, all the while, Miss Grace stood by him, white and still as any stone; and when he had ended she heaved a great sigh, as much as to say her work was done, and her end was accomplished. But the old lord never touched his organ again, and died within the year; and no wonder! for, on the morrow of that wild and fearful night, the shepherds, coming down the Fell side, found Miss Maude sitting, all crazy and smiling, under the holly trees, nursing a dead child, – with a terrible mark on its left shoulder.[22] 'But that was not what killed it,' said Dorothy; 'it was the frost and the cold, – every wild creature was in its hole, and every beast in its fold, – while the child and its mother were turned out to wander on the Fells! And now you know all! and I wonder if you are less frightened now?'

I was more frightened than ever; but I said I was not. I wished Miss Rosamond and myself well out of that dreadful house for ever; but I would not leave her, and I dared not take her away. But oh! how I watched her, and guarded her! We bolted the doors, and shut the window shutters fast, an hour or more before dark, rather than leave them open five minutes too late. But my little lady still heard the weird child crying and mourning; and not all we could do or say, could keep her from wanting to go to her, and let her in from the cruel wind and the snow. All this time, I kept away from Miss Furnivall and Mrs Stark, as much as ever I could; for I feared them – I knew no good could be about them, with their grey hard faces, and their dreamy eyes, looking back into the ghastly years that were gone. But, even in my fear, I had a kind of pity – for Miss Furnivall, at least. Those gone down to the pit can hardly have a more hopeless look than that which was ever on her face. At last I even got so sorry for her – who never said a word but what was quite forced from her – that I prayed for her; and I taught Miss Rosamond to pray for one who had done a deadly sin; but often when she came to those words, she would listen, and start up from her knees, and say, 'I hear my little girl plaining and crying very sad – Oh! let her in, or she will die!'

One night – just after New Year's Day had come at last, and the long winter had taken a turn as I hoped – I heard the west drawing room bell ring three times, which was the signal for me. I would not leave Miss Rosamond alone, for all she was asleep – for the old lord had been playing wilder than ever – and I feared lest my darling should waken to hear the spectre child; see her I knew she could not, I had fastened the windows too well for that. So, I took her out of her bed and wrapped her up in such outer clothes as were most handy, and carried her down to the drawing room, where the old ladies sat at their tapestry work as usual. They looked up when I came in, and Mrs Stark asked, quite astounded, 'Why did I bring Miss Rosamond there, out of her warm bed?' I had begun to whisper, 'Because I was afraid of her being tempted out while I was away, by the wild child in the snow,' when she stopped me short (with a glance at Miss Furnivall) and said Miss Furnivall wanted me to undo some work she had done wrong, and which neither of them could see to unpick. So, I laid my pretty dear on the sofa, and sat down on a stool by them, and hardened my heart against them as I heard the wind rising and howling.

Miss Rosamond slept on sound, for all the wind blew so; and Miss Furnivall said never a word, nor looked round when the gusts shook the windows. All at once she started up to her full height, and put up one hand as if to bid us listen.

'I hear voices!' said she. 'I hear terrible screams – I hear my father's voice!'

Just at that moment, my darling wakened with a sudden start: 'My little girl is crying, oh, how she is crying!' and she tried to get up and go to her, but she got her feet entangled in the blanket, and I caught her up; for my flesh had begun to creep at these noises, which they heard while we could catch no sound. In a minute or two the noises came, and gathered fast, and filled our ears; we, too, heard voices and screams, and no longer heard the winter's wind that raged abroad. Mrs Stark looked at me, and I at her, but we dared not speak. Suddenly Miss Furnivall went towards the door, out into the anteroom, through the west lobby, and opened the door into the great hall. Mrs Stark followed, and I durst not be left, though my heart almost stopped beating for fear. I wrapped my darling tight in my arms, and went out with them. In the hall the screams were louder than ever; they sounded to come from the east wing – nearer and nearer – close on the other side of the locked-up doors – close behind them. Then I noticed that the great bronze chandelier seemed all alight, though the hall was dim, and that a fire was blazing in the vast hearth-place, though it gave no heat; and I shuddered up with terror, and folded my darling closer to me. But as I did so, the east door shook, and she, suddenly struggling to get free from me, cried, 'Hester! I must go! My little girl is there; I hear her; she is coming! Hester, I must go!'

I held her tight with all my strength; with a set will, I held her. If I had died, my hands would have grasped her still; I was so resolved in my mind. Miss Furnivall stood listening, and paid no regard to my darling, who had got down to the ground, and whom I, upon my knees now, was holding with both my arms clasped round her neck; she still striving and crying to get free.

All at once, the east door gave way with a thundering crash, as if torn open in a violent passion, and there came into that broad and mysterious light, the figure of a tall old man, with grey hair and gleaming eyes. He drove before him, with many a relentless gesture of abhorrence, a stern and beautiful woman, with a little child clinging to her dress.

'Oh Hester! Hester!' cried Miss Rosamond. 'It's the lady! the lady below the holly trees; and my little girl is with her.

Hester! Hester! let me go to her; they are drawing me to them. I feel them – I feel them. I must go!'

Again she was almost convulsed by her efforts to get away; but I held her tighter and tighter, till I feared I should do her a hurt; but rather that than let her go towards those terrible phantoms. They passed along towards the great hall door, where the winds howled and ravened for their prey; but before they reached that, the lady turned; and I could see that she defied the old man with a fierce and proud defiance; but then she quailed – and then she threw up her arms wildly and piteously to save her child – her little child – from a blow from his uplifted crutch.

And Miss Rosamond was torn as by a power stronger than mine, and writhed in my arms, and sobbed (for by this time the poor darling was growing faint).

'They want me to go with them on to the Fells – they are drawing me to them. Oh, my little girl! I would come, but cruel, wicked Hester holds me very tight.' But when she saw the uplifted crutch she swooned away, and I thanked God for it. Just at this moment – when the tall old man, his hair streaming as in the blast of a furnace, was going to strike the little shrinking child – Miss Furnivall, the old woman by my side, cried out, 'Oh, father! father! spare the little innocent child!' But just then I saw – we all saw – another phantom shape itself, and grow clear out of the blue and misty light that filled the hall; we had not seen her till now, for it was another lady who stood by the old man, with a look of relentless hate and triumphant scorn. That figure was very beautiful to look upon, with a soft white hat drawn down over the proud brows, and a red and curling lip. It was dressed in an open robe of blue satin. I had seen that figure before. It was the likeness of Miss Furnivall in her youth; and the terrible phantoms moved on, regardless of old Miss Furnivall's wild entreaty, – and the uplifted crutch fell on the right shoulder of the little child, and the younger sister looked on, stony and deadly serene. But at that moment, the dim lights, and the fire that gave no heat, went out of themselves, and Miss Furnivall lay at our feet stricken down by the palsy – death-stricken.

Yes! she was carried to her bed that night never to rise again. She lay with her face to the wall, muttering low but muttering alway: 'Alas! alas! what is done in youth can never be undone in age! What is done in youth can never be undone in age!'

THE HOST'S STORY
[by Edmund Ollier]

Once on a time (as children's stories say),
A merchant came from countries far away
Back to his native land, bearing, conceal'd
In a small casket, diamonds that would yield
A sum sufficient to redeem a king
Taken by force in perilous combating.
This merchant in his trade had now grown old;
And all the chambers of his heart were cold,
And the pale ashes of the fires of youth
Lay on his soul, which knew not joy nor ruth:[23]
But, at a bargain he was sharp and hard,
For cent. per cent. alone he had regard.
To swell his profits, or some mite to save,
He would have seen his children in their grave,
If children he had had; but, like a stone,
He seem'd all self-complete, and bloodless, and alone.
The love of money burnt in him like thirst:
His soul gaped for it, as, when earth is curs'd
With drouth, it gapes for water; and whene'er
He saw a merchant with an equal share,
He long'd to seize on all, by force or stealth,
Adding still more to his preposterous wealth.

Behold him, now, upon the salt sea strand!
Once more he treads upon his native land.
He knows the cliffs along the tawny beach;
He knows, far off, the winding river-reach:
He sees familiar sights – he hears familiar speech.
He stops. Perhaps from off his arid brain

The years have roll'd, and he is young again:
Perhaps, with an emotion strange and new,
The sense of home is on his heart like dew. –
Alas! not so. His only present sense
Is how to lodge tonight without expense.

He wander'd up into the little town;
And there by chance he heard of the renown
Of a great merchant-prince, who lived hard by
In royal pomp and liberality.
With these words carv'd above the open door: –
'Welcome to all men! Welcome, rich and poor!'
Thither that miser gladly turn'd his face,
And soon beheld, within a pleasant place
Beset with leaves that talk'd across the breeze,
White gleams of marble quivering through dark trees;
And, going nearer, saw rich walls arise,
With many windows, sparkling forth like eyes,
And sculptured figures, gazing from a height,
Like travelling angels pausing in their flight,
And colonnades in far-withdrawing rows,
And golden lamps in shadowy porticoes,
And terrace-walks upon the level roof,
Safe from intrusion, quiet, and aloof: –
Such was the palace which this merchant found.

From out the gates there came a restless sound
Of instruments of music; on light wings
Seeming to poise, and murmur of far things
In some divine and unknown tongue to all.
The sordid merchant pass'd into the hall,
And saw the master sitting at the board,

And cried aloud: 'Oh, fair and princely lord:
Behold a ruin'd merchant at thy feet,
Who of thy bounty craves a little meat,
Lest Hunger fang[24] him in the open ways.
Unto thy grace and charity he prays,
And bends him low.' – The host rose up, and took
The merchant by the hand, with genial look,
And welcomed him with smiles and hearty speech,
And, with his own hand, meat and drink did reach,
And fed him nobly. But the miser's eye
Regarded all things avariciously;
And soon the splendours of that sun-bright house, –
Prodigal wealth, and riches marvellous,
The lucid gold, outshining everywhere,
The jewels, making star-rays through the air, –
Kindled a sudden hell-flame in his heart,
Bating his breath, making his blood to start,
And whisper'd in his brain a Devilish thing:
Even this: 'When all the house is slumbering,
And eyes and ears, with fumes of feasting drenched,
Are sealed in sleep and every sense is quenched,
I will arise and seize on what I may,
And place it safely in the court till day;
And, that I may escape with all entire,
This princely house will I consume with fire,
And burn the phoenix in his spicy nest.'

  The feast being done, all rose to seek their rest;
And that old traitor, with his lips of fraud,
Said to the host: 'Sweet sir! a spirit flawed
Has, by the oil and honey of your love,
Been rendered whole; and He who reigns above

Will, I doubt not, increase your righteous store –
Perhaps this very night will crowd still more
Into your chests. Look not incredulously:
Heaven works in darkness and in sleep; and I
Feel that my tongue has spoken prophecy.'

   The host made answer in a courteous tone;
And now the guests into their rooms are shown,
And mirth and light have vanished from the hall,
And sleep lies heavy on the souls of all –
All but that murderous thief, who sits and stares
Into the lamp's broad flame, that idly flares,
Shaking the shadows like a ghostly hand.
He thinks upon the scheme which he has plann'd:
He listens to the stillness round about:
He hears the stirring of the wind without,
The chirping of the crickets far beneath,
The sighing sedge[25] upon the neighbouring heath.
He takes his lamp, and stealthily he goes;
The silent house seems conscious in repose:
Along the stairs the shadows shift and glide;
They cling like shrouded devils at his side:
The marble columns, in their spectral white,
Come heavily through the glooms to meet the light:
A dreary quiet lies upon the place.
That living Avarice, with his crafty face,
Enters the hall, deserted now and cold,
And fills a bag with jewels and with gold,
And takes whatever pleases him the best;
Then places his own diamonds with the rest,
And in the courtyard stows all privily.

Now, wake, ye sleepers; for there's Murder nigh!
A devil is in the house who, while you sleep,
About the basement noiselessly doth creep,
And makes a fire with faggots and with straw;
And soon the flames will gather strength, and flaw
Those solid stones, and wrap them like a cloak,
And glare and lighten through their night of smoke!
Even now the terror hath advanced its head:
The infant mischief carefully is fed:
A scorching tongue hath fastened on the walls –
Farewell the joy! Farewell the festivals!
Up, through the beams, the sharp flames gnaw and break,
Out at the window peering like a snake;
The massive pillars fiercely are embraced;
The leaden conduits slowly melt and waste;
Forth leaps the nimble fire, and hastily
Its bloody writing scores upon the sky!
Forth leap the flames; forth rush the sparks o'erhead;
Forth rolls the smoke, and burns to heavy red;
Forth bursts the steady glare, – and all the night has fled!

A sense of fire has gone throughout the house.
The host, the guests, and all the servants, rouse;
And from their rooms tumultuously they pour,
A wild and stumbling crowd, and through the door
Pass into the courtyard. They look around,
And see their dwelling as with serpents wound,
And weep, and wring their hands, and cry 'Alas!'

Meanwhile, the spoiler, seeking to amass
More treasure still, goes groping here and there
In empty chambers, and all places where

The fire has not yet reached; until at last
He hears the house awake, and knows his chance is past.
He cries aloud, 'I am undone – undone!'
And towards the threshold he attempts to run,
And meets the vengeful fire upon the way,
And glares against its glare, and stands at bay.
It is the master now, and he the slave!
He flies before it; his lips moan and rave;
He runs about; he traces to and fro;
He calls for help; he knows not where to go;
He gnashes like a wild beast in a cage.
The cruel flames come roaring in their rage,
And scorch his robe. He howls, 'I cannot flee!
The fire which I have kindled, eateth Me!'
The pavements glow; the hot air sings and flares;
For very life he dashes up the stairs,
And runs toward a window at the back,
And far away beholds the cloudy rack
Weltering like blood. One chance alone he sees:
He leaps straight out and falls between the trees.
Half-stunn'd, and bruis'd, he rises yet again,
Making strange sounds, and cursing in his pain.
He reels and stumbles, yet still holds his flight,
And fades away into the distant night.

   The noise and clamour have at length awoke
The neighbours round, who see the glare and smoke,
And rise, and cast up water on the flames;
And soon the fierce destruction shrinks and tames.
Back goes the scarlet light from far and nigh;
Back comes the natural darkness to the sky.
The empty windows, with their inward red,

Glow like strange eyes within a dusky head,
And gleam, and glance, and lingeringly die out.
Then, with a joyful cry, the hasty rout[26]
Enter the house, and find the larger part
Whole, and unhurt; and each man in his heart
Rejoices, and makes merry at the sight.
And now the master of that palace bright
Looks round, and finds his household all are there,
Safe from the fire, uninjured in a hair,
Except that aged merchant: only he
Is absent; and no traces can they see,
Although they search the empty rooms and all
The smoking ruins huddled 'gainst the wall.
They think – 'He did not wake in time to fly;'
Till in a heap of charr'd wood they descry
His lamp, and see that there the fire began,
And say among themselves – 'This was the man
Who lit the flames that might have been our death!'
And at that instant, in the self-same breath,
Some others in the open courtyard find
The plunder which the wretch had left behind;
And lo! the store is wondrously increas'd
By a small box of diamonds of the East,
In value greater than a prince's crown.

A proclamation was sent up and down
The neighbouring land, to see if any claim
Were made upon these gems; but no one came.
The true possessor durst not reappear,
To make his title to the jewels clear;
And so, in time, they rightfully belong'd
To him who had so grievously been wrong'd

By the first owner: and their worth was higher,
A thousand fold, than what was burnt by fire.

Thus joy was born out of calamity;
And that old merchant, when he meant to lie,
In very truth had spoken prophecy.

THE GRANDFATHER'S STORY
[by Reverend James White]

When I first took my seat as a clerk in our Bank, the state of the country was far less safe than it is now. The roads were not only unconscious of Macadam,[27] and fatal in many places to wheels and springs, but dangerous to a still more alarming degree from the outrages and robberies to which travellers were exposed. Men's minds were unsettled by the incidents of the war on which we had just entered;[28] commerce was interrupted, credit was at an end, and distress began to be discovered among whole classes of the population who had hitherto lived in comfort. However harshly the law was administered, it seemed to have no terrors for the evildoer, and, indeed, the undiscerning cruelty of the Statute book defeated its own object by punishing all crimes alike. But, a time of pecuniary pressure is not a bad season for a bank. The house flourished, though the country was in great straits; and the enormous profits at that time realised by bankers – which enabled them to purchase large estates and outshine the old territorial aristocracy – made the profession as unpopular among the higher classes as it had already become among the unreasoning masses. By them, a banker was looked upon as a sort of licensed forger, who created enormous sums of money by merely signing square pieces of flimsy paper; and I am persuaded the robbery of a bank would have been considered by many people quite as meritorious an action as the dispersal of a bank of coiners.[29] These, however, were not the sentiments of us bankers' clerks. We felt that we belonged to a mighty corporation, on whose good will depended the prosperity of half the farms in the county. We considered ourselves the executive government, and carried on the business of the office with a pride and dignity that would have fitted us for Secretaries of State. We used even to walk the streets with a braggadocio air, as if our pockets were loaded with gold; and if two of us hired a gig for a country excursion, we pretended to look under the driving seat as if to see to the safety of inconceivable amounts of money: ostentatiously examining our pistols, to show that we were determined to defend our treasure or die. Not seldom these precautions were required in reality; for, when a pressure for gold occurred among our customers, two of the most courageous of the clerks were despatched with the required amount, in strong leathern bags deposited under the seat of the gig, which bags they were to guard at the risk of their lives. Whether from the bodily strength I was gifted with, or from some idea that as I was not given to boasting, I might really possess the necessary amount of boldness, I do not know, but I was often selected as one of the guards to a valuable cargo of this description; and as if to show an impartiality between the most silent and the most talkative of their servants, the partners united with me in this service the most blustering, boastful, good-hearted and loud-voiced young gentleman I have ever known. You have most of you heard of the famous electioneering orator Tom Ruddle – who stood at every vacancy for county and borough, and passed his whole life between the elections, in canvassing for himself or friends. Tom Ruddle was my fellow clerk at the time I speak of, and generally the companion of my drives in charge of treasure.

'What would you do,' I said to Tom, 'in case we are attacked?'

'Tell ye what!' said Tom, with whom that was a favourite way of beginning almost every sentence, 'Tell ye what! I'll shoot 'em through the head.'

'Then you expect there will be more than one?'

'I should think so,' said Tom; 'if there was only one, I'd jump out of the gig and give him a precious licking. Tell ye what! 'Twould be a proper punishment for his impertinence.'

'And if half a dozen should try it?'

'Shoot 'em all!'

Never was there such a determined custodier as the gallant Tom Ruddle.

One cold December evening we were suddenly sent off, in charge of three bags of coin, to be delivered into customers' hands within ten or twelve miles of the town. The clear frosty sky was exhilarating, our courage was excited by the speed of the motion, the dignity of our responsible office, and a pair of horse-pistols[30] which lay across the apron.

'Tell ye what!' said Tom, taking up one of the pistols and (as I afterwards found) full-cocking it, 'I should rather like to meet a few robbers. I would serve them as I did those three disbanded soldiers.'

'How was that?'

'Oh! it's as well,' said Tom, pretending to grow very serious, 'to say nothing about these unfortunate accidents. Blood is a frightful thing on the conscience, and a bullet through a fellow's head is a disagreeable sight; but – tell ye what! – I'd do it again. Fellows who risk their lives must take their chance, my boy.'

And here Tom put the other pistol on full cock, and looked audaciously on both sides of the road, as if daring the lurking murderers to come forth and receive the reward of their crimes. As to the story of the soldiers, and the fearful insinuations of a bloody deed executed on one or all, it was a prodigious rhodomontade[31] – for Tom was such a tender-hearted individual, that if he had shot a kitten it would have made him unhappy for a week. But, to hear him talk, you would have taken him for a civic Richard the Third, one who had 'neither pity, love, nor fear.'[32] His whiskers also were very ferocious, and suggestive of battle, murder, and ruin. So, he went on playing with his pistol, and giving himself out for an unpitying executioner of vengeance on the guilty, until we reached the small town where one of our customers resided, and it was necessary for one of us to carry one of the bags to its destination. Tom undertook this task. As the village at which the remaining parcels were to be delivered was only a mile further on, he determined to walk across the fields, and join me after he had executed his commission. He looked carefully at the priming of his pistol, stuck it ostentatiously in the outside breast pocket of his great-coat; and, with stately steps, marched off with the heavy money bag in his hand. I put the whip to the horse, and trotted merrily forward, thinking nothing whatever of robbery or danger, in spite of the monitory conversation of Tom Ruddle.

Our first customer resided at the outskirts of the village – a farmer who required a considerable amount in gold. I pulled up at the narrow dark entrance of the lane that led up to his house; and, as my absence couldn't be for more than a few minutes, I left the gig, and proceeded up the lane with my golden treasure. I delivered it into the hands of its owner; and, manfully resisting all his hospitable invitations, I took my leave, and walked rapidly towards the gig. As I drew near, I perceived in the clear starlight a man mounted on the step, and groping under the seat. I ran forward, and the man, alarmed by my approach, rapidly raised himself from his stooping position, and, presenting a pistol, fired it so close to my eyes that the flash blinded me for a moment; the action was so sudden and my surprise so great, that for a short time too I was bewildered, and scarcely knew whether I was alive or dead.

The old horse never started at the report, and I rested my hand on the rim of the wheel, while I endeavoured to recover my scattered thoughts. The first thing I ascertained was that the man had disappeared. I then hurriedly examined under the seat; and, to my intense relief, perceived the remaining money bag still in its place. There was a slit in it, however, near the top, as if made by a knife – the robber probably resolving merely to possess himself of the coin, without the dangerous accompaniment of the leathern sack, by which he might have been traced.

'Tell ye what!' said a voice close beside me, as I concluded my scrutiny; 'I don't like practical jokes like that – firing off pistols to frighten folks. You'll alarm the whole village.'

'Tom,' I said, 'now's the time to show your courage. A man has robbed the gig – or tried to do it – and has fired at me within a yard of my face.'

Tom grew perceptibly pale at this information. 'Was there only one?'

'Only one.'

'Then the accomplices are near. What's to be done? Shall we rouse farmer Malins and get his men to help?'

'Not for the world,' I said, 'I would rather face a dozen shots than have my carelessness known at the Bank. It would ruin me for life. Let us count the money in this bag, quietly deliver it if it be correct, and then follow the robber's course.'

It was only a hundred guinea bag, that one, but the counting was nervous work. We found three guineas wanting. We were luckily able to supply them from our own pockets (having just received our quarter's salaries), and I left Tom there, delivered the bag at its destination very near at hand, without a word of the robbery, and went back to him.

'Now! Which way did he go?' said Tom, resuming a little of his former air, and clutching his pistol like the chief of a chorus of banditti in a melodrama.

I told him I had been so confused that I had not observed which way he had retreated. Tom was an old hand at poaching – though he was a clergyman's son, and ought to have set a better example.

'I have heard a hare stir at a hundred yards,' he said, and laid his ear close to the frosty ground. 'If he's within a quarter of a mile, I shall hear him move.' I lay also down on the ground. There was silence for a long time. We heard nothing but our breathing and the breathing of the horse.

'Hush!' said Tom at last. 'He has come out of hiding. I hear a man's step far away to the left; bring your pistol, and let us follow.' I took the pistol and found the flint down on the pan.[33] The man had fired at me with my own weapon, and no wonder he had fired so suddenly; for Tom now acknowledged to his belief that he had forgotten to uncock it.

'Never mind,' said Tom, 'I'll blow his brains out with mine, and you can split his skull with the butt end of yours. Tell ye what! It's of no use to spare those malefactors. I'll fire, the moment I see him.'

'Not till I tell you whether it is the robber or not.'

'Should you know him, do you think?'

'In the flash of the powder I saw a pair of haggard and amazed eyes which I shall never forget.'

'On, then!' said Tom; 'we'll have a three hundred pound reward, and see the rascal hanged besides.'

We set off, slowly and noiselessly, in the direction Tom had pointed out. Occasionally he applied his ear to the ground, and always muttering 'We have him! we have him!' proceeded in the same careful manner as before. Suddenly Tom said,

'He's doubling. He has been leading us on the wrong scent all this time; he has turned towards the village.'

'Then our plan,' I said, 'should be to get there before him. If we intercept him in that way, he can't escape; and I feel sure I could identify him if I saw him by candlelight.'

'Tell ye what! – that's the plan,' replied my companion. 'We'll watch at the entrance of the village, and arrest him the moment he comes in.'

We crept through an opening of the hedge, and got once more in the straight lane that led to the village. It was now very late, and the cold was so intense that it kept every person within doors; for, we heard no sound in the whole hamlet, except, high up in the clear air, the ticking of the church clock, and the loud jangle of the quarters that seemed like peals of artillery in the excited state of our minds and senses. Close to the church – which appeared to guard the entrance of the village, with its low buttressed walls, and its watchtower of a steeple – there was a wretched ruined-looking cottage, which projected so far into the lane that the space between it and the church was not more than eight or nine feet. It struck us both at the same moment that if we could effect a lodgement here, it was impossible for the man to slip into the village without our observation.

After listening for a while at the windows and doors of the building, we concluded it was uninhabited; gently pushing open the door, we climbed a narrow stone staircase, and were making for a gable end window which we had observed from the road, and which commanded the whole approach to the village, when we heard a voice say in a whisper, as we attained the garret we were in search of, 'Is that you, William?'

We stopped for a minute or two and the speaker's expectation was disappointed. We now placed ourselves at the window, and listened for the slightest sound. We remained there, listening, for a long time. Several quarters had died off into 'the eternal melodies,' far up in the church tower, and we were just beginning to despair of seeing the object of our search, when Tom nudged me noiselessly with his elbow.

'Tell ye what!' he whispered very softly, 'there's a footstep round the corner. See! There's a man under the hedge looking up at the next window. There – he moves! We must be after him. Hallo! Stop – he crosses the lane. He's coming into this very house!'

I certainly did see a figure silently steal across the road and disappear under the doorway of the building we were in. But, we had no light; and we knew nothing of the arrangement of the rooms. Another quarter thrown off from the old church clock, warned us that the night was rapidly passing away. We had almost resolved to retrace our steps if possible, and get back to where we had left our unfortunate horse, when I was again nudged by my friend's elbow.

'Tell ye what!' he whispered. 'Something's going on;' and he pointed to a feeble glimmer on the rafters of the roof above us.

The light proceeded from the next room, which had not been built up above the height of the ceiling joists, so that the roof was common to both chambers – the adjoining one, and that in which we were – the partition wall being only seven or eight feet high. We could have heard anything that was said, but we listened in vain for the slightest sound. The light, however, continued to burn; we saw it flickering across the top of the habitation, and dimly playing far up among the dark thatch of the roof.

'Tell ye what!' said Tom. 'If we could get up, on these old joists, we could see into the next room. Hold my pistol till I get up and – tell ye what! – then I can shoot 'em easy.'

'For Heaven's sake, Tom!' I said, 'be careful. Let me see whether it is the man.'

'Come up, then,' said Tom, who now bestrode one of the main beams and gave me a hand to aid my ascent. We were both on the level of the dividing wall, and, by placing our heads a little forward, could see every portion of the neighbouring room. A miserable room it was. There was a small round table, there were a couple of old chairs; but utter wretchedness was the characteristic of the cheerless and fireless apartment.

There was a person, apparently regardless of the cold, seated at the table and reading a book. The little taper which had been lighted without any noise, was only sufficient to throw its illumination on the features and figure of the reader, and on the table at which she sat. They were wasted and pallid features – but she was young, and very pretty; or the mystery and strangeness of the incident threw such an interest around her, that I thought so. Her dress was very scanty, and a shawl, wrapped closely round her shoulders, perhaps displayed, rather than concealed the deficiency of her clothing in other respects. Suddenly we saw at the farther end of the room a figure emerge from the darkness; Tom grasped his pistol more firmly, and put the cock back, preventing it from making any noise with his thumb. The man stood in the doorway, as if uncertain whether to enter or not. He looked for a long time at the woman, who still continued her reading; and then silently advanced. She heard his step, and lifted up her head, and looked in his face without saying a word. Such a face, so pale, so agitated, I never in my life saw.

'We shall go tomorrow,' he said; 'I have got some money as I expected.' And with these words he laid three golden guineas on the table before her. Still, she said nothing – but watched his countenance with her lips apart.

'Tell ye what!' said Tom; 'That's the money. Is that the man?'

'I don't know yet, till I see his eyes.' In the meantime, the conversation went on below.

'I borrowed these pieces from a friend,' continued the man, as if in answer to the look she bent on him; 'a friend, I tell you. I might have had more, but I would take only three. They are enough to carry us to Liverpool, and, once there, we are sure of a passage to the West. Once in the West, the world is before us. I can work, Mary. We are young – a poor man has no chance here, but we can go to America with fresh hopes – '

'And a good conscience?' said the woman, in a whisper like Lady Macbeth's.

The man was silent. At last he seemed to grow angry at the steadiness of her gaze. 'Why do you look at me in that manner? I tell you we shall start tomorrow.'

'And the money?' said the woman.

'I will send it back to my friend from whom I borrowed it, out of my first earnings. I took only three, in case it should incommode him to lend me more.'

'I must see that friend myself,' said Mary, 'before I touch the money.'

'Tell ye what! Is it the man?' again asked Tom.

'Hush!' I said; 'let us listen.'

'I recognised a friend of mine in one of the clerks in the Melfield Bank. I give you my word I got the coins from him.'

'Tell ye what! He confesses,' said Tom; 'let us spring on him by surprise – an ugly ruffian as ever I saw!'

'And with that sum,' he continued, 'see what we can do. It will relieve us from our distress, which has come upon us – Mary, you know I speak the truth in this – from no other fault of mine than too much confidence in a treacherous friend.

I can't see you starve. I can't see the baby reduced from our comfortable keeping to lie on straw at the end of a barn like this. I can't do it – I won't!' he went on, getting more impassioned in his words. 'At whatever cost, I *will* give you a chance of comfort and independence.'

'And peace of mind?' replied Mary. 'Oh, William, I must tell you what terrible fears have been in my heart, all this dreary night, during your absence; I have read, and prayed, and turned for comfort to Heaven. Oh, William, give the money back to your friend – I say nothing about the loan – take it back; I can't look at it! Let us starve – let us die, if it must be so – but take that money away.'

Tom Ruddle gently put down the cock of his pistol, and ran the sleeve of his coat across his eyes.

'Let us trust, William,' the woman went on, 'and deliverance will be found. The weather is very cold,' she added. 'There seems no visible hope; but I cannot altogether despair at this time of the year. This barn is not more humble than the manger at Bethlehem, which I have been reading about all night.'

At this moment, a great clang of bells pealed from the old church tower; it was so near that it shook the rafters on which we sat, and filled all the room with the sharp ringing sound. 'Hark!' cried the man, startled, 'What's that?' – 'It is Christmas morning,' said the woman. 'Ah, William, William, what a different spirit we should welcome it with; in what a different spirit we *have* welcomed it, many and many a happy time!'

He listened for a moment or two to the bells. Then he sank on his knees, and put his head on her lap; and there was perfect silence except the Christmas music. 'Tell ye what!' said Tom. 'I remember we always sang a hymn at this hour, in my father's house. Let us be off – I wouldn't disturb these people for a thousand guineas.'

Some little noise was made by our preparations to descend. The man looked up, while the woman still continued absorbed in prayer. My head was just on the level of the wall. Our eyes met. They were the same that had flashed so wildly when the pistol was fired from the gig. We continued our descent. The man rose quietly from his knees, and put his finger to his lip. When we got downstairs he was waiting for us at the door. 'Not before *her*,' he said. 'I would spare her the sight, if I could. I am guilty of the robbery, but I wouldn't have harmed you, sir. The pistol went off, the moment I put my hand upon it. For God's sake tell her of it gently, when you have taken me away!'

'Tell ye what!' said Tom Ruddle – whose belligerent feelings had entirely disappeared – 'the pistol was my mistake, and it's all a mistake together. Come to my friend and me, at the Bank, the day after tomorrow, and – tell ye what! – the sharp wind brings water to my eyes – we'll manage to lend you some more.'

So, the bells still rang clear in the midnight air; and our drive home through the frosty lanes was the pleasantest drive we ever had in our lives.

THE CHARWOMAN'S STORY
[by Edmund Saul Dixon]

A person is flustered by being had up into the dining room for to drink merry Christmases and them (though wishing, I am sure, to every party present as many as would be agreeable to their own selves), and it an't easy rightly to remember at a moment's notice what a person *did* see in the ghostly way. Indeed I never seen nothing myself, it being Thomas which did so – and *he* heard it. Hows'ever, the account of it having been seemingly carried to the young ladies by Nurse, and they wishing to know it all correct, it were as I will now mention.

I was cook to Alderman Playford when he died so suddenly; and very handsome mourning we servants had, though I'm only a hard-working charwoman now.

The Alderman kept up two establishments; his town house at Dewcester, for the sake of the business, and his country house at Brownham, five or six miles off. I was at Brownham, and I liked that the best because the young ladies liked it best; they were real ladies, they were. We had everything comfortable there; I may say grand: gardens, there was, and fish ponds, a brewery, and a dairy, besides stables and that. Latterly too, the Alderman spent most of his time there. Thomas, the coachman, used to drive him backwards and forwards when he had to go to Dewcester; where he sometimes slept, if there was anything particular going on in the Aldermen's Room, or if there was a Ward Election coming on; for the Alderman, you know, was a great electioneerer. But Thomas always came home to us: when the Alderman slept at Dewcester, he returned to Brownham for the sake of protection to us females, and to attend to the things.

Now the Alderman had had a paralytic stroke some years before; and, ever since then, though he got quite over it, he had a very curious step, and one of his shoes made a queer creaking noise, not like any other noise as ever I heard. As he used to be coming down the front gravel walk, or going from one part of the house to another – it was a large, old-fashioned, red brick house, it was – his shoe went 'Creak! creak!' so that you could tell exactly where he was without seeing him. He didn't walk heavy, and he didn't walk quick; and, long before he came in sight, you knew he was a coming by the noise of his creaking shoe, though you couldn't hardly hear the sound of his footsteps. I've heard many and many a creaking shoe, but I never heard one creak like that.

Thomas and me was very good friends. I thought he'd meant more by it than he did, though I don't believe, even now, that 'twas all cupboard love, though certainly some of it was. Who can tell what might have happened, if he hadn't married the Widow Rogers, that everybody said was left so well, when she wasn't? Poor Thomas! The day after his wedding was a sad day for him; he having gone and done it, past looking back. But we was always good friends at Brownham, as fellow servants ought to be. I was mistress in the kitchen; and he didn't fare the worse for that.

One evening he'd come back from driving the Alderman to Dewcester, and he was to go and fetch him in the afternoon next day. The night was wet and muggy, with a gusty wind. As we sat in the kitchen, we could hear the rain beat against the outside shutters, and the water pour from the spouts on the roof. The wind puffed and blew, like a man in a passion, as if it were whirling round and round the house, to try and find a place to get in at. Thomas had taken off his wet leggings and things, and put on his indoor ones, and we all sat chatting round the kitchen fire a little later than usual. We heard the young ladies go upstairs to bed, and then the other maids went up to bed too, leaving Thomas and me a little while to ourselves.

So we went on talking and talking about the family, and about the neighbours, and I thought that, perhaps, Thomas would say something about his feelings; but he was just as usual. When the kitchen clock pointed to a quarter to twelve, I took up my candle, and says, 'Good night, Thomas, I'm going to bed.' – 'Good night, cook,' says he; 'I'll clear away the ladies' supper things out of the dining room, and then I'll go to bed, too, for I'm tired,' says he.

I hadn't been upstairs more than a quarter of an hour, and hadn't finished undressing, before I heard someone tapping at my door. 'Who's that?' says I, in a fright. – 'That's me, cook,' says Thomas, 'I want to speak to you.' – I couldn't think what he wanted to say; he'd had plenty of time to say anything particular, but I little thought he'd seen the Widow Rogers that very afternoon. So I dressed myself, and came out into the passage, and there stood Thomas looking more serious than I'd ever seen him at church. 'Come downstairs, cook,' says he, 'I've something to tell you;' so solemn-like that I couldn't think what could be the matter.

We went into the kitchen. I made up the fire a little, and sat down by it. Thomas took a seat on the other side. He behaved just as if he'd been at a funeral. 'Cook,' says he, 'I'm sure you'll hear of something soon.' – 'Lor, Thomas,' says I, 'what should I hear of?' – 'Why,' says he, 'you'll find the Alderman is dead.' – 'Dead!' says I, 'that's very shocking!'

'It isn't half so shocking as what *I* have just heard. Cook,' says he, in a hollow tone of voice, 'Cook, I have just heard the Alderman's ghost, and I'm sure we shall never see him any more alive! When I went to clear away the ladies' supper things in the dining room, I found a glass full of punch standing in the middle of the tray. You know that's the way they often do, when I come home wet after driving the Alderman' – (for they were *real* ladies: it would have been too familiar-like to say, Thomas, here's a glass of punch for you) – 'and I was just going to drink it off to the Alderman's health, when I heard the hall door open, and creak! creak! creak! came the sound of his footsteps across the hall. I did not at the moment think it strange he should come back to Brownham so late, and so I sets down the punch, and takes up a candle, and runs out of the room, to show him a light. I could see nothing at all; but master's footsteps passed me, and went creak! creak! creak! up the stairs. I followed them to the first landing place, but still I could see no Alderman, nor nothing. I cries out 'Good God, sir, where are you? Don't do this!' I stopped and listened; not a sound but the creak! creak! creak! The footsteps went up to his room door; I heard the door open and shut, and then I heard nothing more. But, cook, the doors are all barred and locked for the night, and how could the Alderman get into the house? As sure as you're alive, I've heard his ghost!'

I thought so too, at the time, and now I know it. We sat up all night to be ready for the news when it came from Dewcester. Early next morning a messenger arrived. Thomas let him in; and *before* he told us what had brought him to Brownham, Thomas said to him, 'Alderman Playford is dead.' The messenger was astonished, as well he might be, and said 'Lor, how could *you* know that?' – 'He died last night,' said Thomas, 'as the clock was striking twelve, and I heard his footstep cross the hall, and go up the staircase. The Alderman's step is like nobody else's, and I knew by that he must be dead.'

And wishing we may all live happy ever afterwards!

THE DEAF PLAYMATE'S STORY
[by Harriet Martineau]

I don't know how you have all managed, or what you have been telling. I have been thinking all this time, what I could tell that was interesting; and I don't know anything very particular that has happened to me, except all about Charley Felkin, and why he has asked me to go and stay there. I will tell you that story, if you like.

You know Charley is a year younger than I am, and I had been at Dr Owen's a year when he came. He was to be in my room; and he did not know anything about school; and he was younger, and uncomfortable at first; and altogether, he fell to my share; and so we saw a great deal of each other. He soon cheered up, and could stand his ground; and we were great friends. He soon got to like play, and left off moping; and we used to talk a great deal in wet weather, and out on long walks. Our best talks, though, were after we were gone to bed. I was not deaf then; and we used to have such talks about home, and ghosts, and all sorts of things; and nobody ever overheard us that we know of, but once; and then we got nothing worse than a tremendous rap at the door, and the Doctor bidding us go to sleep directly.

Well; we went on, just so, for a good while, till I began to have the earache. At first, Charley was very kind to me. I remember his asking me, once, to lean my head on his shoulder, and his keeping my head warm till the pain got better; and he sat quite still the whole time. But perhaps he got tired; or – I don't know – perhaps I grew cross. I used to try not; but sometimes the pain was so bad, and lasted so long, that I used to wish I was dead; and I dare say I might be cross enough then, or dismal, which boys like worse.

Charley used to seem not to believe there was anything the matter with me. I used to climb up the apple tree, and get on the wall, and pretend to be asleep, to get out of their way; and then the boys used to come running that way, and say, 'Humpty Dumpty sat on the wall;' and one day when I heard Charley say it, I said 'Oh, Charley!' and he said, 'Well, why do you go dumping there?' and he pretended that I made a great fuss about nothing. I know he did not really think so, but wanted to get rid of it all. I know it, because he was so kind always, and so merry when I got well again, and went to play with the rest. And then, I was pleased, and thought I must have been cross, to have thought the things I had; and so we never explained. If we had, it might have saved a great deal that happened afterwards. I am sure I wish we had.

When Charley came, he was a good deal behind me – being a year younger, and never having been to school. I used to think I could keep ahead of all but three boys in my class; and I used to try, hard, to keep ahead of them. But, after a time, I began to go down. I used to learn my lessons as hard as ever; still, somehow the boys were quicker in answering, and half a dozen of them used to get my place, before I knew what it was all about. Dr Owen saw me, one day, near the bottom of the class; and he said he never saw me there before; and the usher said I was stupid; and the Doctor said, then I must be idle. And the boys said so too, and gave me nicknames about it; I even thought so myself, too, and I was very miserable. Charley got into our class before I got out of it; and indeed I never did get out of it. I believe his father and mother used to hold me up to him – for he might easily speak well of me while he was fond of me. At least, he seemed bent upon getting above me in class. I did try hard against that; and he saw it, and tried his utmost. I could not like him much then. I dare say I was very ill-tempered, and that put him out. After I had tried till I was sick, to learn my lesson perfect, and then to answer questions, Charley would get the better of me; and then he would triumph over me. I did not like to fight him, because he could not have stood up against me: and besides, it was all true – he did beat me at lessons. So we used to go to bed without speaking. We had quite left off telling stories at night, some time before. One morning, Charley said, when we got up, that I was the most sulky fellow he ever saw. I had been afraid, lately, that I *was* growing rather sulky, but I did not know of any particular reason that he had for saying so just then (though he had a reason, as I found out afterwards). So, I told him what I thought – that he had grown very unkind, and that I would not bear with it if he did not behave as he used to do. He said that whenever he tried to do so, I sulked. I did not know, then, what reason he had to say that, nor what this was all about. The thing was, he had felt uncomfortable, the night before, about something in his behaviour to me, and he had whispered to me, to ask me to forgive him. It was quite dark, and I never heard him: he asked me to turn and speak to him; but I never stirred, of course; and no wonder he supposed I was sulking. But all this is very disagreeable; and so I will go on to other things.

Mrs Owen was in the orchard one day, and she chanced to look over the hedge, and she saw me lying on my face on the ground. I used often to be so then, for I was stupid at play, where there was any calling out, and the boys used to make game of me. Mrs Owen told the Doctor, and the Doctor said there must be something wrong, and he should be better satisfied if Mr Pratt, the surgeon, saw me. Mr Pratt found out that I was deaf, though he could not tell what was the matter with my ears. He would have put on blisters, and I don't know what else; but the Doctor said it was so near the holidays, I had better wait till I got home. There was an end to taking places, however. The Doctor told them all, that it was clear now why I had seemed to go back so much; and that he reproached himself, and wondered at everybody – that the reason had not been found out before. The top of the class was nearest to the usher, or the Doctor, when he heard us; and I was to stand there always, and not take places with the rest. After that, I heard the usher very well, and got on again. And after that, the boys, and particularly Charley, were kinder again; and if I had been good-tempered, I dare say all would have gone right. But, somehow, everything seemed to go wrong and be uncomfortable, wherever I might be, and I was always longing to be somewhere else. I was longing now for the holidays. I dare say every boy was longing for the holidays; but I was particularly, because everything at home was so bright, and distinct, and cheerful, compared with school, that half-year. Everybody seemed to have got to speak thick and low; most of the birds seemed to have gone away; and this made me long more to see my turtle doves, which Peggy had promised to take care of for me. Even the church bell seemed as if it was muffled; and when the organ played, there were great gaps in the music, which was so spoiled that I used to think I had rather there had been no music at all. But all this is disagreeable too; so I will go on about Charley.

His father and mother asked me to go home with him, to stay for a week; and father said I might; so I went – and I never was so uncomfortable in my life. I did not hear what they said to each other, unless I was quite in the middle of them, and I knew I looked stupid when they were all laughing, and I did not know what it was about. I was sure that Charley's sisters were quizzing me, – Kate particularly. I felt always as if everybody was looking at me; and I know they talked about me sometimes. I know it because I heard something that Mrs Felkin said one day, when there was a noise in the street, and she spoke loud without knowing it. I heard her say, 'He never told us the poor child was deaf.' I don't know why, but I could not bear this. And, after that, some of them were always telling me things in a loud voice, so that everybody turned and looked at me; and then I made a mistake sometimes about what they told me; and one mistake was so ridiculous that I saw Kate turn her back to laugh, and she laughed for ever so long after. Altogether, I could not bear it, and so I ran away. It was all very silly of me, and I know I was very ill-tempered, and I know how Mr and Mrs Felkin must have found themselves mistaken about me, as a friend for Charley; but I did not see any use in staying longer, just to be pitied and laughed at, without doing any good to anybody; so I ran away at the end of three days. I did so long to come home; for I never had any doubt that everything would be comfortable at home. I knew where the coach passed, – a mile and a half from Mr Felkin's, – very early in the morning, and I got out of the study window and ran. Nobody was up, though, and I need not have been afraid. I had to ask the gardener for the key of the back gate, and he threw it to me from his window. When I was outside, I called to him to bid him ask Charley to send my things after me to my father's house. By the roadside, there was a pond, under a high hedge, and with some dark trees bending over it. It just came into my head to drown myself there, and I should be out of every body's way, and all this trouble would be at an end. But ah! when I saw our church steeple, I was happy! When I saw our own gate, I thought I should go on to be happy.

But I did not. It was all over directly. I could not hear what my mother whispered when she kissed me; and all their voices were confused and everything else seemed to have grown still and dull. I might have known all that; but somehow I did not expect it. I had been vexed that the Felkins called me deaf; and now I was hurt at the way in which my brothers and sisters used to find fault with me for not hearing things. Ned said once 'none are so deaf as those that won't hear;' and my mother told me, every day, that it was inattention; that if I were not so absent, I should hear as much as anybody else. I don't think I was absent. I know I used to long and to try to hear till I could not help crying; and then I ran and bolted myself into my own room. I think I must have been half crazy then, judging by what I did to my turtle doves. Peggy had taken very good care of them; and they soon knew me again, and used to perch on my head and my shoulder, as if I had never been away. But their cooing was not the least like what it used to be. I could not hear it at all, unless I put my head against the cage. I could hear some other birds very well; so I fancied it must somehow be the fault of the doves that they would not coo to me. One day I took one of them out of the cage, and coaxed her at first, and tried every way; and at last I squeezed her throat a little. I suppose I got desperate because she would not coo as I wanted; and I killed her – broke her neck. You all remember about that – how I was punished, and so on: but nobody knew how miserable I was. I will not say any more about that: and I would not have mentioned it but for what it led to.

The first thing that it led to, was, that the whole family were, in a way, afraid of me. The girls used to slink away from me; and never let me play with the baby – as if I should strangle that! I used to pretend not to care for being punished; and I know I behaved horridly. One thing was – a very disagreeable thing – that I found father and mother did not know

94

everything. Till now, I had always thought they did: but, now, they did not know me at all; and that was no great wonder, behaving as I did then. But they used to advise things that were impossible. They used to desire me to ask always what everybody said: but we used to pass, every Sunday, the tombstone of old Miss Chapman; and I remembered how it used to be when anybody saw her coming in at the gate. They used to cry out 'O dear, here comes Miss Chapman! What *shall* we do? She will stay till dinner time, and we shall not get back our voices for a week. Well! don't tell her all she asks for. She is never satisfied. Really it is a most dreadful bore,' and so on, till she was at the room door. This was because she *would* know everything that everybody said. I could not bear to be like her; and I could not bear now to think how we all used to complain of her. It was only from a sort of feeling then that I did not do what my father and mother told me, and that I was sure they did not understand about it: but now, I see why, and so do they. One can't tell what is worth repeating and what is not. If one never asks, somebody always tells what it is best to tell; but if one is always asking and teasing, people must get as tired of one as we were of poor Miss Chapman.

So, I had to get on all alone. I used to read in a corner, great part of the day; and I used to walk by myself – long walks over the common, while the others used to go together to meadows, or through the lanes. My father commanded me to go with the rest; and then I used to get another ramble by myself. There was a pond on the common, so far like that one in the lane I spoke of, that it put me in mind of what I mentioned. I used to sit and look into the pond and throw stones in. I began to fancy, now, that I should be happier when I got back to school again. It was very silly when I had once been so disappointed about home; but, I suppose everybody is always hoping for something or other – and I did not know what else to hope. But I keep getting into disagreeable things and forgetting Charley.

One night when the elder ones were just thinking of going to bed, I came down in my nightclothes, walking in my sleep with my eyes wide open. The stone hall, so cold to my bare feet, awoke me; but yet I could not have been quite awake, for I went into the kitchen instead of up to bed again, and I remember very little about that night. They say I stared at the candles the whole time; but I remember Dr Robinson being there. I seldom slept well then. I was always dreaming and starting, – dreaming of all sorts of music, and of hearing the wind, and people talking; and then of all sorts of trouble from not being able to hear anybody; and it always ended with a quarrel with Charley, and my knocking him down. But my mother knew nothing of this, and she was as frightened that night as if I had been crazy. The Doctor advised them to send me to school again for one half-year, and see how I got on after some experiments had been tried with my ears. But I want to get on about Charley.

Charley arrived at school, two hours after me. He seemed not to like to shake hands, and he walked away directly. I saw he did not mean to be friends; and I supposed he felt his father's house insulted by my running away. But, I did not know all the reason he had, – neither then, nor for some time after. When we became friends again, I found that Kate had seen how hurt I was at her laughing at me, and that she was so sorry that she went up to my room door several times, and knocked, and begged that I would forgive her; or that I would open my door, and speak to her, at least. She knocked so loud that she never doubted my hearing her; but I never did, and the next thing was that I ran away. Of course, Charley could not forgive this; he was my great enemy now. In school, he beat me, of course; every body might do that: but I had a chance in things that were not done in class, – such as the Latin essay for a prize, for instance. Charley was bent upon getting that prize, and he thought he should, because, though he was younger than I, he was a good deal before me in school. However, I got the prize; and some of the boys said it was a shame. They thought it was through favour, because I had grown stupid. They said so, and Charley said so; and he provoked me all he could, – more on Kate's account than his own, though, as he told me afterwards. One day, he insulted me so in the playground, that I knocked him down. There was no reason why I should not now; for he had grown very much, and was as strong as I had ever been, while I was nothing like so strong as I had been, or as I am now. The moment he was up, he flew at me in the greatest rage that ever you saw. I was the same: and we were hurt enough, I can tell you, – both of us, – so much, that Mrs Owen came to see us in our own rooms (for we had not the same room this half-year). We did not want to tell her anything, or to seem to make a party. But she somehow found out that I felt very lonely, and was very unhappy. I am sure it was her doing that the dear, considerate, wise Doctor was so kind to me when I went into the school again, – being very kind to Charley too. He asked me, one afternoon, to go for a drive with him in his gig. The reason he gave was, that his business took him near the place where my father and he used to go to school together; but I believe it was more that we might have a long talk, all by ourselves.

We talked a good deal about some of the fine old heroes, and then about some of the martyrs; and he said, what to be sure is true, that it is an advantage for any one to know clearly, from beginning to end, what his heroism is to be about, that he may arm himself with courage and patience, and be secure against surprises. I began thinking of myself; but I did not suppose *he* did, till it came out by degrees. He thought that deafness and blindness were harder to bear than almost anything. He called them calamities. I can't tell you all he said: he never meant that I should: but he told me the very worst; and he said that he did it on purpose. He told me what a hopeless case he believed mine to be, and what it would cut me off from; but, he said that nothing of the sort could cut a person off from being a hero, and here was the way wide open for me: not for the fame of it, but for the thing itself. I wondered that I had never thought of all that before; but I don't think I shall ever forget it.

Well! When we came back, there was Charley loitering about, – looking for us, clearly. He asked me whether we should be friends. I was very willing, of course: and it was still an hour to supper; so we went and sat on the wall under the apple tree, and talked over everything. There, we found how much we had both been mistaken, and that we did not really hate one another at all. Ever since that, I have liked him better than ever I did before, and that is saying a great deal. He never triumphs over me now; and he tells me fifty things a day that he never used to think of. He says I used to look as if I did not like to be spoken to; but that I have chipped up wonderfully. And I know that he has given up his credit and his pleasure, many a time, to help me, and to stay by me. He will not have that trouble at school again, as I am not going back; but I know how it will be at Charley's home, this time. I know it, by his saying that Kate will never laugh at me again. I believe she might, for that matter. At least, I think I could stand most people's laughing, now. Father and mother, and everybody, know that the whole thing is quite altered now, and that

Charley and I shall never quarrel again. I shall not run away from that house again, – nor from any other house. It is so much better to look things in the face! How you all nod, and agree with me!

THE GUEST'S STORY
[by Samuel Sidney]

About twenty years ago, I was articled clerk in the small seaport town of Muddleborough, half rural, half fishing, with a small remains of once profitable smuggling, and a few reminiscences of successful privateering, to which one street and several public-houses[34] owed their foundation. The rector, the banker, the lawyer – my master, who had the tin cases of half the county, in the dusty dining room that formed his office – the doctor, and the owner of the two brigs and a schooner which composed the mercantile navy, were the acknowledged heads of our town.

It was a moot point whether the banker or my master, the lawyer, were the greater man. The banker, Isaac Scrawby, was supposed to be of boundless wealth; it was before the time of Joint-stock Banks,[35] and there was not a farmer or a fisherman who did not prefer Scrawby's torn, dingy notes, to the newest Bank of England. His paper was the stock of canvas bags, and was hoarded away in old women's worsted stockings; as was plainly shown when he stopped payment in the first crisis after Peel's Bill,[36] and paid three shillings in the pound. But then, Lawyer Closeleigh, my master, besides being able to lend everybody money, knew all the secrets of the county, and had a hand in everything – except the births, which he left to the doctor.

There were three or four clerks who jog-trotted through the business. Old Closeleigh generally wore a green coat with gilt basket buttons: breeches, and top-boots; seldom sat down or took up a pen except to write a letter to a great client; but held audiences on market days, and gave advice, and took instructions at coverside in the hunting season.

As a large premium had been paid with me, of course I did nothing; an attempt was made while I was yet green, by old Foumart, the common law clerk, to induce me to serve writs; but, that having failed, I was left to take care of one of the rooms of the deserted mansion which formed our offices, and to entertain the clients who were shown in to wait their turn.

Dulness and respectability were the characteristics of our town. We had few poor, or if we had, we never heard much about them. The same people went through the same duties and the same serious amusements, all the year round. The commencement of the fishing season, and the annual fair, were our only events. There were no fortunes made or lost. Smuggling, under the modern arrangements, had become too hazardous and low for respectable people to venture on, although there were strange stories afloat, as to the adventures of the fathers of the present generation.

Every year, the more restless and ambitious young men of all classes swarmed away to regions where industry was more active. In a word, 'our town' was the quietest, sleepiest collection of plodding, saving, non-speculating folks, whose utmost efforts enabled them to keep the town pump in repair, and the roof of the town hall watertight; but, who could never be induced to raise money enough to build a much needed pier, or to remit the town dues, in order to induce a steamboat – a recent innovation which passed our port – to call in and open up competition with the slow sailing coasters on which we were dependent for communication with the next town.

Into this English Sleepy Hollow, there came one day – whether by land or water, in a fishing boat, or on his sturdy legs, never was known – a tall, thin, pale, bronzed, soldier-like looking man, between forty and fifty years of age: with one hand, and an iron hook screwed on a wooden block where his other should have been; scantily dressed in a half-soiled, half gamekeeper suit.

A party, including the parson, the doctor, and my master, Mr Closeleigh, were going out shooting over a famous wood-cock cover, and were lamenting aloud the absence of old Phil Snare – the best beater[37] in the county – when the one-armed man offered his services, in a manner so neat, civil, and respect-ful, that, although there was a slight taste of brogue in his accent, and ours was a county where wandering Irishmen were not held in much favour, they were accepted. A long hazel wand was soon in his hand; and, before the day was over, it was universally acknowledged that one-handed Peter was the best beater, and the most amusing handy fellow, that any of the party had ever known. According to his story, he was a pen-sioned soldier proceeding to visit a relation whom he hoped to find well settled at a town a hundred miles to the north. A glass of grog opened his mouth, and he related with great tact a few of his adventures.

From that day, Peter became the odd man of the town, and every one wondered how we had done so long without so useful a personage. He carried letters, he cleaned guns, he manufactured flies for fishing, he doctored dogs, he brought the messages of wives – wrapped in a droll envelope of his own – to dilatory husbands delaying at club dinners; he took the place of the doctor's boy and the lawyer's, too; was always ready with a grave face and a droll answer; was never tired, and seldom in a hurry. He walked in and out of all houses like a tame cat, and made a capital living, as all people do who manage to become the indispensable solvers of difficulties.

In a very short time Peter had emerged, a very butterfly, from the grub or chrysalis state. The ragged shooting jacket was discarded for a green coat of loose fit and many pockets, smart enough for my Lord Browse's head gamekeeper. An open waistcoat displayed highly respectable linen; from head to foot he showed the advantage of being on good credit with the best tradesmen; and yet he owned no master. He began to give up carrying messages, except for the 'fust of the quality;' had a staff of boys, to whom he gave orders; and, when out on a shooting party, carried a capital gun – the property of a sporting publican – with the air of one who came out purely for health, exercise, and sport; and not the least like the half-starved ragged creature who had been too happy to sleep in a barn, and accept a plate of broken meat.

But, the favour in which Peter was held was not confined to our sportsmen; he seemed equally taken into the confidence of those who never handled a gun or threw a fly. He began with the smallest tradesmen, but grew daily more indispensable to our most topping shopkeepers. Mr Tammy, the draper in the marketplace, who always wore a white cravat and pumps, was seen walking in his garden with Peter for an hour one evening, by Miss Spark, who peeped through a hole in the garden door; and she declared that Peter at parting patted Tammy on the back – yet he was churchwarden that year! This story was at first disbelieved, although it was remarked that Peter's improvement in hosiery dated from that garden walk. Soon afterwards, Kinine, our head chemist and druggist, a great orator at parish meetings, and a scientific authority, was observed by his errand boy studying geography, with a large map before him: over which Peter's iron hook travelled with great rapidity. From that time, the whole town seemed seized with a rage for refreshing its geographical studies. Spain and Portugal were the special localities in favour; the demand for books on the Peninsular War[38] became great at the circulating library; and the bookseller in the market received orders for not less than three Portuguese dictionaries, in one week.

As for Peter, he became a lion of the first magnitude. He breakfasted with Smoker, the sporting publican – dined with Tiles the shoemaker – took tea with Jolly the butcher – supped with Kinine the druggist – and held chats with Smooth the barber, and Mr Closeleigh himself. Ostensibly, he was asked to relate the stories of his campaigns, which he did with great unction; and, strangely enough, people never seemed tired of hearing of Peter's marches, Peter's battles, and how Peter lost his hand. It was remarked by the curious, that these battle stories always ended in Peter's being taken mysteriously into some back parlour or garden, there to whisper for an hour or two with the head of the house over a pipe and strong waters; though no one ever saw Peter the worse for liquor. No, Peter always seemed to imbibe silence with his grog.

At length, in spite of very vigorous attempts at mystery, it began to be whispered about, that Peter was the owner of a valuable secret concerning a treasure buried in the wars. People not yet in his confidence pooh-poohed the idea, and yet Peter's friends increased in number daily.

For my own part, I had not yet arrived at the money hunting age; my heart was then all upon horses and dogs, embroidered waistcoats, and Albanian fancy dresses: with some dreams of Gulnares and Medoras,[39] and pretty Annie Blondie, the rector's daughter. A hidden treasure did not excite me to desire Peter's patronage, nearly so much as his skill in dressing a Mayfly. As it happened, my passion for fishing let me into the secret which had been travelling up and down the best streets of our town.

One fine summer's evening I had been trying all I knew, without success, to inveigle a great four pound trout, who kept lazily rising and sinking at the far side of a deep pool, under the overhanging roots of a gnarled willow tree; when Peter, stealing with his quiet lengthy stride across the grass, made his appearance at my elbow suddenly.

'Will you let me try, Master Charles, what I can do with the big rogue?'

I did let him, and he dropped the fly – a fly of his own making – just behind the big trout, as light as thistle-down; one dash, one splash; and in ten minutes the trout was safe under my landing net, flapping out his life on the grass.

'Always throw just behind them big 'uns, Master Charles, and they'll take sure enough, but they won't look at a fly just before them. Same as rich men for that!' added Peter, with a chuckle.

This triumph over the trout led the way to chat on the grass, and, little by little, we got at last to Peter's battles in Spain and Portugal. I cannot do justice to Peter's oily flattery, and the sympathy he expressed for a raal gintleman and a sportsman: not like the poor mean beggars of peddling shopkeepers. He made me understand that I was one who would spend money in true style if I had it; and then, after hinting that a beautiful young lady in the neighbourhood had confided to Peter – every one did confide in Peter – her preference for Master Charles, with many artful roundabouts he confided to me the following story; the key to the favour he had acquired among all ranks of the good people of Muddleborough.

Peter declared that during the retreat to Torres Vedras, he and two other comrades were entrusted with the care of a waggon laden with boxes of gold doubloons; that in a skirmish they had retreated for safety to a convent, and there tilted the waggonload, all but one box, into a deep convent well. The same day, all his companions were killed in action, and he was wounded and laid in the hospital. At this point of his story he exhibited a ghastly scar in his side.

The one box they had partly divided amongst them, and partly buried. He had, on recovery, been sent to join his regiment, and marched to the Pyrenees and Toulouse: where he lost his hand. On his arrival in England he was discharged with a pension (here he produced papers); he had after long trials succeeded in getting back to Portugal; he had found the convent deserted, and the well half filled with rubbish; he had discovered, too, the small parcel of doubloons, but found that it would require the influence of some real gentleman to get the treasure out of the well, and out of the country. When his romance had proceeded thus far, he produced from some recondite part of his garments, wrapped in many rags, a real golden doubloon.

Who could disbelieve so circumstantial a story, supported by so much evidence? He went on to say that the publican, the druggist, the shoemaker, the gunsmith, and many others, were all anxious to go in partnership, and start for Portugal; that Mr Tammy was willing to advance something handsome on the speculation; but that he preferred dealing with a young gentleman of spirit, and that if I could persuade my rich aunt to advance the money necessary for the journey – a trifle of two hundred pounds – he was willing to give up the handsome offers of Tammy, Kinine, Tiles, Smoker, and all the rest of them; and set out with me, secretly and alone, to rifle this new cave of Aladdin. His plans were very complete. We were to hire a vineyard – part of the old convent grounds – and, after getting up the treasure, were to pack it in Port-wine casks with double bottoms, and then, returning, share the spoil. I was to marry a beautiful lady, keep a pack of hounds, and be the head of the county; while Peter was modest and would be quite satisfied with enough to maintain a horse, a couple of setters, and the life of a squireen.[40]

The romance was well put together and most insinuatingly told; but, I was rather too young, too indifferent, too merry, and too full of little minor schemes, to bite. Besides, I did not think that my Aunt Rebecca would give me two hundred pounds to go to Portugal with a strange Irishman; and I did not quite like the notion of leaving my favourite Annie Blondie to the exclusive care of my rival, the young curate. So, after giving Peter my honour that I would not reveal the momentous secret to any living soul, we parted at the Fisherman Tavern: where I paid for divers glasses of grog, and presented Peter with the only half-sovereign I was likely to have that week.

In the course of the month Peter was missing. It was observed that all his patrons – Smoker, and Tiles, Jolly, Kinine, and Tammy – looked particularly pleased and mysterious when they heard others wonder at his disappearance without beat of drum.

About a week after Peter's departure, Mrs Jolly went to Mrs Smoker to know if she had seen anything of her husband. Mrs Smoker had not. Had Mrs Jolly seen anything of that brute Smoker? The two wives compared notes: both husbands had been selling and raising money. Smoker had raffled his favourite mare Slap Bang, and Jolly had collected all his largest Midsummer bills, and taken her (Mrs Jolly's) grandfather's silver tankard. Both had packed up their Sunday clothes, saddles, and guns. There was a terrible hue and cry, which was not mollified when letters came from the two absconding husbands – one dated London, and the other Liverpool – stating that they had only gone to make their fortunes by a safe speculation, and would be back in three months. Peter had been suspected; but, what was odd, they both asked after Peter, and desired –

the one, that he might have the run of the ale tap; the other, that he might have a bit of beef or mutton if he wanted it.

In the midst of the hubbub, Peter got down one morning from the top of the coach from the neighbouring town of Fuddleborough, and crept into the midst of the gossips at the Horse and Jockey before they were aware of him. His story was very short and straightforward; he had only been to draw his pension; and he had seen Jolly at the Theatre Royal Covent Garden very drunk, but had not spoken to him. In less than an hour he was closeted with Kinine, and he spent the evening with the Churchwarden.

In another week it was announced that Mr Kinine had sold his business, and was leaving the town for good. Some said he was going to study for a physician; some said he had inherited – others said he was ruined. At any rate he left, and was never seen at Muddleborough any more. The last time I heard of him he was lecturing on Electro-Biology – or anything else – admittance twopence.

Very oddly, on the same week in which Kinine gave up to his successor, Bluster, who still keeps the establishment, Tammy the Churchwarden went off to Manchester – to buy goods, as he said, although it was not his time of the year for buying. He left the shop in charge of young Binks, who afterwards married Mrs Tammy. Tammy was away, six months; during the whole of which period poor Mrs Tammy claimed to be distracted; and when he came back he was 'as thin as a weasel, as bald as a coot, and as yellow as a guinea.' So Miss Spark declared; but very few people saw him, for he took to his bed and died: raving about treasure waggons, and the villain Peter, and doubloons. The day he was buried, it all came out. Tammy had been to Portugal with Peter; who, after travelling up the country, had handed him over to the police as a heretic spy, and had departed with mules, baggage, and all the money that was to have been spent on the vineyard, the casks with double bottoms, the waggons, and the rest of the complete arrangements.

Poor Tammy, when discharged, had almost to beg his way to Oporto;[41] and there, the first person he saw was Kinine, inquiring at the police office for the scoundrel Peter, who, after a jollification in London had marched off with his trunks and bank bills – the produce of his business – to join Tammy.

When poor Mrs Tammy told this tale at the funeral breakfast, the murder came out. Peter had bamboozled the whole village. Everybody, from the cobbler to the parson, had made an investment in the Portuguese treasure well. Smoker went through the Gazette; Jolly had to discharge his journeyman and do his own killing; every one had paid something for listening to Peter's stories. He had swept the old women's stocking hoards, and the servant girls' riband savings; he had had fifty pounds and some tracts from the Rector, and twice as much, and a new gun from Mr Closeleigh. The banker had given him a hundred pounds in his own one-pound notes. The village schoolmaster had lent him his only five pounds. In fact, he found our town a perfect bank of credulity, and he had drained it dry.

But Peter had committed no legal offence: he had only told lies and borrowed money. I heard of him from time to time, always as being successful, until a few years ago, when he made the mistake of taking a keen American whom he picked up in a railway carriage, to Oporto. On this occasion, the American came back and Peter did not. When asked after his friend, the American composedly remarked, 'That having had a difficulty with Peter, he had been obliged to shoot him.'

THE MOTHER'S STORY
[by Eliza Griffiths]

The traveller, of reverend mien,
A wanderer from his youth had been;
Dwelt in the desert and the wood,
Escaped from earthquake, fire and flood;
And each dark point, each vivid hue,
    That lay on his wild pilgrimage,
Had melted to a moonlight view –
    A quiet, beautiful old age.
And travel to his heart had brought
A worldwide stretch of kindly thought,
Had given his recollecting eye
Almost the tone of infancy.
And he could make the cheek turn pale,
Yet better loved some gentle tale
    Of love and truth to tell,
O'er which his heart refreshed would stay,
As traveller on some dusty way
    Might linger by a well.
And such a tale the ancient man
Here, at our fireside once began: –

It was my lot, 'mid Western woods,
To form a friendship firm and dear;
How oft in those vast solitudes
A friend is sooner found than here!
It was a youth of noble blood
Who chose, in his romantic mood,
    In hunter's hut to dwell;
A gifted youth of bearing high,

A free, proud step, a glancing eye –
      His name was Claude d'Estrelle.
His heart had found him one who made
  Those solitary places glad;
A hunter's orphan – left, while young,
Her Indian mother's tribe among –
Who saw him dying on the waste,
And on her fearless bosom placed
His fevered head, and touched his brow
With hands as cool and soft as snow;
And when, at his first conscious waking,
      He saw his guardian of the woods,
In whose dark eye a hope was breaking
      Like moonlight over dusky floods,
While tears of mingled joy and doubt
      Down from the heavy lashes ran,
As though her heart was flowing out
      In pity for the lonely man –
His mov'd soul vowed that maiden brave
Should own the life she tried to save.
So Leena, ere that summer fled,
The noble Claude d'Estrelle had wed.

On one of those red autumn eves –
      That gorgeous time of forest life –
Amid its wealth of changing leaves
      I first beheld my friend's young wife.
We met upon an open glade,
Whence lines of brown and purple shade
Their long, soft swelling vistas made
      Up to the evening sky.
And, while we gazed, some dim arcade

Would kindle suddenly,
And gleaming orange grove o'er grove
Seem vying with the clouds above:
While crimson foliage, here and there,
Would deepen in the amber air,
And drops of glory fall between
On many a glistening evergreen;
The waterfall to jewels turned,
The lake like one great ruby burned
    Upon the wood's green breast;
And all that 'wildering splendour seemed
As still as something we had dreamed;
The leaf's light flutter to the ground
Became a noticeable sound,
    So silent was its rest!
And Leena's figure, lithe and tall,
    Against the glowing background stood: –
Well might her husband ask if all
The dames that tread in courtly hall
    Could match his lady of the wood;
There, wearing for her coronet
Her own rich bands of wavy jet;
    Soft as the fawn's her eye,
A colour on the clear brown cheek
Like evening's last faint crimson streak
    Upon the twilight sky.
Long, pleasant nights with Claude I passed
In his rude dwelling on the waste,
    Beside the fire of pine:
While Leena's graceful tenderness
Wreathed round him like the light caress
    Of her own forest vine;

And love's strange magic seemed to shut
A palace in that woodland hut,
While we would stop our talk, to hear
The distant rushing of the deer,
The sound of falling water near;
And Leena, happy as a child,
Brought for us from her native wild
    The gatherings of her heart:
Soft gushes of melodious thought
Deep poetry within her wrought,
    By living long apart.
While Claude's bright smiles fell fond and fast
Upon his dear enthusiast,
And, all untrained, he loved to find
Those blossoms of the uncultured mind,
And thought not how the world might try
    The spirit of his untaught wife,
Though all who looked on Leena's eye
Might feel some destined agony
    Lay folded in her life.
Such a high power of deathless love
Did in its depths unfathomed move;
It seemed for special trials given,
The boon of a foreseeing Heaven.

That time of trial came at last,
When five delightful years had passed,
    And I had wandered wide.
A second time Claude laid to rest
His sick head on that faithful breast;
    So rested till he died.
Then she unto his brother went,

With those his dying breath had sent –
Her children twain, a welcome prize –
    The last of that proud race.
But there were none but scornful eyes
For her woe-printed face;
And back he harshly bade her go,
That those she bore might yet outgrow
    The sense of her disgrace.
What! leave them; Claude's dear legacy!
How could she let the mother die
    In such a loving heart?
But, with an uncomplaining eye,
    (Despair had taught her art),
She begged a little while to stay,
And stole them in the night away,
    And hid them in the wood;
Seven days and nights, was sorely pressed,
And then, beside her rifled nest,
    A childless mother stood!
But when her love's strong crying still
Did too much chafe the iron will,
He gave her, with an ample bribe,
Unto a stranger Indian tribe
    A slave oppressed to be;
For there her white blood was her shame;
But woman's heart, whate'er her name,
Indian, or English, is the same –
    A mother set her free.
She tracked them to a distant state
    By many a wild and dangerous way,
And prayed the tyrant of her fate
    That she, among his slaves, might stay

Near her beloved ones, though she bore
A mother's precious name no more.
He suffered her to take her part
    Upon the slave's tear-watered soil;
So little knew the mother's heart,
    He thought to tire it out by toil.
But, stronger than the strong man's will,
Her children's love would own her still.
He felt the taint must on them lie
Till he had quenched her memory,
So secretly he sent her where
'Neath Afric's hot unwholesome air
    A wild plantation lay;
A fearful place of toil and tears,
Where, how she lived for twenty years,
    Sure only God might say.
To cheer her lonely banishment
A dream of Claude He nightly sent,
And of the little children too;
(For in her heart they never grew).
Oh, what sick thoughts wore out her prime!
The long, long wasting of the time!
The dark hair changed, the eyesight dim
    Had spent itself in tears;
But still her firm and patient hope
Grew stronger as each slender prop
    Fell from it with the years;
And o'er her love, time harmless fled;
Absence but nursed it, tears but shed
A rainbow glory on its head;
And hardship, pain, and cruelty,
Proved it, to find it could not die.

Her life did but one thought contain –
To see her children once again.
For twenty years she strove, and then
   At last she reached the shore;
Heaven put it in a sailor's heart
To let her in his ship depart,
   And seek her lost, once more.

She reached home with the closing year;
Oh, had they died, those children dear?
Had they forgotten? No! not *her*!
To them she begged her way along;
Her earnest purpose made her strong;
Some careless strangers gave her ear
News that it burned and thrilled to hear;
How, when years past, her old foe died,
Another childless brother tried
To bring her children to his side;
And how her son right gladly went
Into his forest settlement.
Some said he lived a hunter wild,
And some that he had died a child.
Then of her daughter; – she had stayed
   The treasure of her wealthy home,
And grown so beautiful, they said.
   Enough! For nought she has not come.
The high heart throbs, the dark eyes fill;
Then one at least is living still!

Anon, beside a lady fair
   Stood Leena in a splendid room;
Gazed on the curls of auburn hair,

The lustrous eyes, the flushing bloom,
With half a sigh to think how wild
Her fancy, that a little child
   Might meet her at the door,
That might be petted and caressed,
And nestle in its mother's breast,
   As in the days of yore.
And yet 'twas with a joyful thrill
Of pride she saw her beauty still.
'Leena!' She does not turn as though
It was her name. Poor mother, no!
Alas for thee! that cold surprise,
   So unbelieving, so unmoved –
How can she, with her father's eyes,
   Look strangely on the face he loved?
The little dream child she hath lost –
   And yet may no new daughter find?
It cannot be; she hath a host
   Of memories to wake her mind.
Sure she has but to prove her claim!
She knows not yet the mother's name.
She clasped her knees, to melt her pride
With Love's pathetic questions tried,
Pausing between them to espy
Some little softening in the eye.
Had she not seen the eyes before her
At childish wakings bending o'er her?
Had not these hands her baby head
With forest blossoms often spread?
And then that tune – her father's tune!
How it had been her nightly boon,
To hear it as she sank to rest?

An impulse moved the loving breast;
That tune. 'Twas but a lullaby;
But she to turn the air would try,
And nature's sleeping sympathies
Beneath the sweet old notes might rise.
'Twas a quaint fancy as might be,
And born of love's credulity;
That song – oh, how it trembled up!
   It almost seemed a sighing –
The farewell of departing Hope
   While Joy and Love lay dying.
A common tune it scarce could be;
   The heart had set the homely words
To an impassioned melody
   That swept from its excited chords;
That, and the face so grave and meek,
The wistful eye, the changing cheek,
   Made such a touching spell,
The longing hand was fondly laid
Upon her daughter's haughty head,
   And there she let it dwell.
Yea, Childhood's love seemed springing there.
But, hush! a step upon the stair
   That daughter loveth well.
And he, she knows his title high
Would ne'er to Indian blood ally;
Her pride, her love, are all at stake;
She strives the kindly spell to break:
Tells Leena, with some natural pain,
That they must never meet again;
And offers – insult strange and cold –
To buy her secrecy with gold.

The mother fled, as one afraid,
Two days and nights: and never stayed
   Her hot and panting feet.
It was the time of festival,
And doors and hearts were open all,
   And friend with friend did greet.
The light and warmth around her glowed,
While hers was still the frozen road –
   An emblem of her fate.
And yet the broad, unsleeping eye
That guides the sparrows in the sky,
   Did on her footsteps wait.

She sank beneath an oak tree bare,
On the third night, she knew not where.
The pure snow seemed the only thing
To her sick heart's imagining
That had not changed; and she would lie
Upon its quiet breast, and die.

A little further, sinking heart!
   To the next turning only press;
'Tis hard that thou should'st die; thou art
   But one stone's throw from happiness!
Hush! rising on the frosty air,
   It is a Christmas hymn!
The kindly sounds have reached her there;
   Have roused a feeling dim,
Amid the lonesomeness of death,
That someone, on a prayerful breath,
   Her passing soul might bear;
Perhaps through her exhausted frame

Some strong, mysterious impulse came
    From Him who brought her there.
And, in its strength, she dragged her feet
Round to a straggling village street,
    And reached a house of prayer.
She saw not how red men and white,
(The sudden glow, the glare of light,
    Those heavy eyes made blind),
Were stirring, 'neath the breath intense
Of one young preacher's eloquence
    Like corn before the wind.
At last the listless ear was met
    By one consoling word:
'A mother; yea, *she* may forget:
    I will not, saith the Lord.'
And, from the preacher's lips there sprung
The grand poetic Indian tongue,
The while his reaching fancy strove
To paint that holiest earthly love –
A mother's; and he told a tale
So like her own it made her veil
Her eyes, lest, with a look at him,
She might dispel a blissful dream.
And, as her ear the rich voice drank,
A wild hope, with it, rose and sank,
And thus unto an end he drew:
'Her fate, oh, would to God I knew!

    Alive, or dead, I cannot tell;
But well I know that mother's love
Here pining, or at peace above,
    Hath not forgotten Claude d'Estrelle!'
She made no cry, she heard the name;

A little lower sank her head:
A gentle pause of being came,
   And well it did, or life had fled.
No other words, nor prayer, nor hymn,
   Nor gathering feet the long trance broke,
Till, with each sense confused and dim,
   At last upon his arm she woke,
And saw compassion soft and warm
   Rain o'er her from his full dark eye,
And felt as one beneath a charm,
   Content for ever thus to lie:
Her heart so weak with the excess
Of its unspoken happiness.
Yet, from her lips his own words fell –
'Hath not forgotten Claude d'Estrelle.'
And then her shaking hand did seek
To part his hair, to touch his cheek;
The voice, the touch, the loving eyes,
Did link up broken memories
   That could not be withstood;
His life with Nature and with Heaven
To him had quick perceptions given:
   His heart was at the flood;
It moved him on, he could not speak,
But, with strong weeping clasped her neck.
And sobbing women, at the scene,
Dropped tear for tear with hardened men:
And e'en the Indians of the wood
Like weeping children round them stood
Till one old thankful heart did stay
The whirl of joy, with 'Let us pray!'
But oh, that quiet, joyful night,

While Claude and his fair girlish wife
Moved round her with such proud delight;
   Now stopped to weep at her past life,
Now gently chafed the blistered feet,
Anon between them moved her seat;
Now, as they sat, the way-worn brow
   Was pressed against the golden hair
Or to the blooming cheek; and now
   Claude's glowing lips were meeting there.
Of Christmas hearths there never shone
A brighter, dearer, happier one.

I heard this story when I came –
   In part from Claude, in part from one
Who called upon her mother's name
With deep remorse and burning shame,
   When friend and hireling all were gone,
And he, who but her gold had wed,
Approached not her infected bed.
Oh, for that one kind face that she
   So harshly drove away!
That sad, heart-breaking melody
   Did haunt her while she lay.
I went for Leena, and she came –
(Hers the true love that does not blame,
   That 'suffers and is kind') –
Touched the parched lips, and knew no fear,
Though Death was kissing them with her;
   Poured on the fevered mind
The dew of her forgiving love,
Till there Heaven's olive branch and dove
   A resting place did find.

And but one fancy did remain –
To hear that cradle hymn again.
And Leena would not that she died
With her last wish ungratified;
So – trembling, through that silent room,
Amid Death's deeply gathering gloom –
Sang with calm lips her fav'rite strain,
But with a heavy heart again:
Full well we knew the closing ear
   Would lose it all too soon;
That she, as its last notes drew near,
   Was dying with the tune.
And when the lullaby had ceased,
We saw she had been sung to rest.

Leena and I met once again.
A pleasant evening, after rain
And storm, her latter life hath been;
I watched her bend her eyes serene
   Upon the Book of Life,
And asked myself could they have seen
   So much of pain and strife?
And children's children unto her
As loving little teachers were;
A very presence from above,
That simple woman's faith and love.

NOTES

1. Located on the Royal Exchange, Garraway's was one of many coffee houses that attracted merchants and other businessmen from the late seventeenth century onwards.

2. A heavy woven cloth of a dark grey colour with white flecks.

3. Completed in 1677, a stone column in East London commemorating the Great Fire of 1666. The Doric column stands 202 feet high, and visitors may climb to a viewing balcony at its top, which also features a copper urn symbolising the fire.

4. Later editions corrected this spelling to 'Jezebel'. The wife of King Ahab in the Old Testament, Jezebel is blamed for the corruption of the Israelites because she persuaded her husband to worship Baal; the name came to be used generally to signify an immodest, deceitful or seductive woman.

5. References to stories in *The Arabian Nights*, one of Dickens' favourite books. Valentine and Orson are the title characters of a popular children's book based on a fifteenth-century romance in which twin brothers are abandoned in a forest. Valentine, raised by the King of France, eventually reunites with and tames Orson, who was reared by a bear.

6. King and queen of the Roman gods (in Greek mythology, Zeus and Hera).

7. 'Prisoners' base' is a game of tag with ancient roots in which children take captured players from the opposing team to a base; the object is to imprison all of the players from the other team. 'Hare and hounds' is a nineteenth-century board game of chase with French origins.

8. Specially decorated cakes served on 6th January, the Twelfth Night after Christmas (also called Epiphany). The person who receives the cake slice containing a coin, bean, or other token is crowned the 'king' or 'queen' of the gathering.

9. Producers of tuns, large casks to hold beer, wine or other liquids.

10. The Klarälven river; the longest river in Sweden.

11. Also *Wanderjahr*, a year of travelling apprenticeship preceding the establishment of one's practice in a trade (German).

12. The uppermost edge of a boat or ship's side.

13. Journeyman (German).

14. To cut and trim the long, narrow pieces of wood that must curve to form the sides of casks, or tuns.

15. Distributors and sellers of coal.

16. An ornately decorated triangle-shaped garment which covered the chest as well as the stomach and was worn under bodice lacing.

17. 1 Peter 1:24. 'For all flesh is as grass, and all the glory of man as the flower of grass. The grass withereth, and the flower thereof falleth away.'

18. A fool or simple-minded person.

19. This character's name inexplicably changes from Agnes to Bessy then back to Agnes; the original variations appear here.

20. A woollen shepherd's plaid, grey in colour and worn especially in southern Scotland.

21. Proverbs 16:18. 'Pride goeth before destruction, and an haughty spirit before a fall.'

22. This reference to a mark on the child's left shoulder appears to be a mistake, as the wound was previously located on the child's right shoulder and is later identified again as having been inflicted upon her right shoulder.

23. Compassion; also sorrow or remorse.

24. Seize or lay hold of.

25. A term for diverse types of grassy, rush-like plants that grow in moist areas.

26. A disorderly crowd or mob.

27. A type of roadway surfacing named after its inventor, Scotsman John Loudon McAdam (1756–1836), who authored the very successful *Remarks on the Present System of Road Making* (1816). Macadamisation improved road surfaces by using a base of slightly graded, drained soil on top of which were laid multiple layers of small, broken stones that would compact and strengthen with the continued weight of passing vehicles.

28. 'The Grandfather's Story' is set in the late eighteenth century, when highwaymen were known to rob and harass travellers; captured bandits were subjected to the death penalty. Britain was engaged in several military actions in the late 1700s, including the American Revolutionary War (1775–83) and ongoing hostilities with France, which culminated in the Napoleonic Wars (1799–1815).

29. Counterfeiters.

30. Large pistols carried by horsemen at the front of the saddle.

31. Boast.

32. Spoken by Richard as he stabs King Henry in William Shakespeare's *Henry VI, Part III* (V.vi.68): 'I, that have neither pity, love, nor fear.'

33. After a flintlock pistol is fired, the flint that functions as ignition rests in the pan that holds the gunpowder. Left in the fully cocked position, such a pistol easily fires.

34. Taverns, usually attached to inns, providing refreshment and/or entertainments for community members and travellers.

35. Banks whose capital is possessed by a large number of stockholders, as opposed to banks controlled by a small number of individuals in partnership.

36. Sir Robert Peel (1788–1850) chaired the 1819 Parliamentary committee that, through a series of legislative reforms, returned Britain to the gold standard in 1821. The new policies resulted in short-term currency crises as local banks had issued an excess of depreciated paper bills.

37. One who rouses game by shaking or striking grass, brush or other places of cover.

38. Waged from 1808–14, after Napoleon seized the throne of Spain in order to install his brother Joseph as king. With aid from Britain, Portugal and Spain ultimately defeated and drove out the French troops.

39. The beautiful Gulnare and Medora are the objects of romantic and chivalric interest in 'The Corsair' (1814) by Lord George Gordon Noel Byron (1788–1824). Extraordinarily popular, the poem's initial print run of 10,000 copies sold out on the first day of its release.

40. Landowner with a small estate.

41. Also called Porto, the second largest city in Portugal and the place for which port wine is named.

BIOGRAPHICAL NOTE

Charles Dickens (1812–70), a true celebrity in the Victorian period, remains one of the most well-known British writers. His most popular works, such as *Great Expectations* (1861) and *A Christmas Carol* (1843), continue to be read and adapted worldwide. In addition to fourteen complete novels, Dickens wrote short stories, essays and plays. He acted on the stage—more than once in amateur theatricals of his own production, and at the end of his life gave a series of powerful public readings from his works. Dickens' journalism is a lesser-known yet central aspect of his life and career. In 1850, he founded *Household Words*, where he worked as editor in chief in addition to writing over one hundred pieces himself. In 1858, after over twenty years of marriage, Dickens abruptly separated from his wife Catherine in order to pursue a relationship with Ellen Ternan, a young actress. A dispute with his publishers, one of whom was representing Catherine in the separation negotiations, caused Dickens to engage in court proceedings over the rights to the name *Household Words*. As a result of winning the suit, Dickens folded *Household Words* into a new journal, *All the Year Round*, in 1859. From 1850–67, Dickens published a special issue of these journals each December that he called the Christmas number. Collaborative in nature, including the work of up to nine different authors, the Christmas numbers were extremely popular and frequently imitated by other publishers. *A Round of Stories by the Christmas Fire* is an early example of what turned into one of Dickens' most profitable endeavours, for the Christmas numbers often sold over 200,000 copies.

Reverend Edmund Saul Dixon (1809–93), rector of Intwood with Kenswich, also published under variations on the pseudonym E.S. (Eugene Sebastian) Delamer. With his wife, he wrote *Wholesome Fare, or The Doctor and the Cook* (1868), 'By Edmund S. and Ellen J. Delamere'. Dixon was an expert on poultry, publishing *Ornamental and Domestic Poultry: Their History and Management* in 1848, an influential text that went into several reprinted editions. Dixon built upon the success of what came to be called 'The Chicken Book' with additional works, such as *The Dovecote and the Aviary* (1851), *Pigeons and Rabbits* (1854) and *Flax and Hemp* (1854). Dixon's pieces for *Household Words* sometimes illustrated his expertise in poultry and horticulture, but also covered other topics, such as 'French National Defences' (1st January 1853) and 'The Ether' (29th May 1858).

Elizabeth Cleghorn Gaskell (1810–65), publishing as 'Mrs Gaskell', was the immensely respected author of several Victorian novels, novellas and short stories. The daughter of a Unitarian minister, she married Reverend William Gaskell in 1832, with whom she had several children, two of whom died in infancy. Gaskell's debut novel, *Mary Barton* (1848), took its protagonists from the working classes in Manchester. After reading the copy Gaskell sent him, Dickens wrote to her that the book 'profoundly affected and impressed him'. An ardent admirer from that point forward, Dickens successfully solicited many contributions from her for *Household Words*. In the first issue, her 'Lizzie Leigh' immediately follows Dickens' 'Preliminary Word'. *Cranford*, one of Gaskell's most popular works, was initially published as a series of sketches in *Household Words* then later printed in book form. Gaskell is also known for writing the first biography of Charlotte Brontë, with whom she was close friends and a regular correspondent. At the request of Brontë's father, Gaskell completed *The Life of Charlotte Brontë* for publication in 1857, just two years after Brontë's death. After some disagreement over Dickens' manner of dividing *North and South* into weekly instalments, Gaskell continued to contribute small pieces to his journals but chose *The Cornhill* for what she thought of as her best work. At the time of her sudden death in 1865, her novel *Wives and Daughters* was left unfinished in the midst of its serialisation in *The Cornhill*.

Eliza Griffiths is called 'Miss Griffith', 'Miss Griffiths', and 'Eliza Griffiths' in the *Household Words* Office Book, but her true identity remains a mystery. In total, this writer contributed twelve poems to the journal between 1850 and 1853.

Harriet Martineau (1802–76) began publishing at the young age of nineteen and became a controversial journalist, novelist, economist, and social reformer for the rest of her life. She also wrote verse and children's books. Martineau reported having a difficult childhood, ruled by a strict mother and plagued by physical maladies. She experienced trouble with her ears from birth and was almost totally deaf by the age of twenty, using an ear trumpet to amplify the little she could hear. When her family faced financial troubles in 1829, she turned to writing as a way to support herself, earning immediate acclaim with *Traditions of Palestine* (1829–30). *Illustrations of Political Economy* (1832–34) cemented her fame. The awkwardly narrated work drew readers from all segments of society even though it was aimed at the working classes in the hopes that increased understanding of political economy would lead to improved relationships between the classes. Martineau also travelled extensively in the United States, widening the scope of her celebrity and exchanging ideas with many of the early feminists who organised the Seneca Falls Convention. Dickens liked her *Society in America* (1837) so much that he asked her to write for *Household Words*, to which she became a regular contributor, particularly in the year of 1852. Beginning in 1853, Dickens and Martineau differed over political economy, Catholicism, and women's rights. They published acrimonious attacks on one another's work and eventually parted ways. Martineau published nothing in *Household Words* after January 1855. Nevertheless, a positive review of her much lauded *Autobiography* – written in just three months as she neared the end of her life – appeared in *All the Year Round* in April of 1877.

Edmund Ollier (1826/7–86), a writer of verse and prose, came from a literary family. His father Charles was a well-known publisher of Romantic writers, such as Leigh Hunt, John Keats and Percy Bysshe Shelley. As a result, Ollier met many renowned literary figures in his childhood, and his poetry was heavily influenced by the Romantics. From 1844 onward, Ollier was a prolific writer, and Hunt himself praised Ollier's verse. In addition to publishing pieces in Dickens' periodicals, *The Magazine of Art,* and *Ainsworth's Magazine*, Ollier held various journalistic positions, including an editorship at *The Atlas* and a literary editorship at *The London Review*. He also published several works of history for Cassell, including *Cassell's History of the War between France and Germany* (1871–2) and *Cassell's Illustrated Universal History* (1881–5).

Samuel Sidney (1813–83) was the permanently adopted pseudonym of Samuel Solomon. After working for a brief time as a solicitor, Sidney turned to the profession of writing and published on a wide array of subjects. *Railways and Agriculture in North Lincolnshire* (1848) and *Rides on Railways* (1851) were followed by a series of pieces on emigration to Australia, many of which appeared in *Household Words*. His novel *Gallops and Gossips in the Bush of Australia* (1854) was dedicated to Dickens, who admired it. From 1847–57, he was a correspondent for *The Illustrated London News*, and from 1850–1, he acted as an assistant commissioner for the Great Exhibition. In addition to writing a column called 'Horse Chat' for *The Live Stock Journal*, he also managed several horse shows. Sidney collected his extensive knowledge of horse breeding, riding and management in *The Book of the Horse* (1873), which remained popular for decades.

William Moy Thomas (1828–1910) was a prolific journalist who contributed to several periodicals in addition to serving as the first editor of *Cassell's Magazine*. Early in his career, he was the private secretary of Charles Wentworth Dilke, a liberal politician and proprietor of *The Athenaeum*. Thomas edited *The Poetical Works of William Collins* (1858) as well as *The Letters and Works of Lady Mary Wortley Montagu* (1861). A staff member of *The Daily News* from 1868–1901 and correspondent for *The New York Round Table* from 1866–67, he was also a drama critic and novelist. Thomas' novel *A Fight for Life* was published in *Cassell's* in 1868. Dickens respected Thomas' work highly, and Thomas was a vice president of the Dickens Fellowship after Dickens' death.

Reverend James White (1803–62) was one of Dickens' close friends and a frequent contributor to his journals as well as to *Blackwood's Magazine*. After leaving his post as vicar of Loxley in Warwickshire, White was able to reside on property his wife Rosa had inherited on the Isle of Wight. From 1839 onward, he did much of his writing from the Isle. Born in Midlothian and educated for a time at Glasgow University, White's heritage inspired him to write Scottish historical tragedies, such as *Feudal Times* (1847). Dickens called *The Earl of Gowrie* (1845) 'a work of most remarkable genius', and White later dedicated *John Savile of Haysted* (1847) to Dickens. White also wrote historical accounts, including *The Eighteen Christian Centuries* (1858), which went into multiple editions in the first years of it printing.

Melisa Klimaszewski is a Visiting Assistant Professor at DePauw University, where she specialises in Victorian literature, world literature, and critical gender studies. She has published articles on nineteenth-century servants and is now pursuing a book-length project that focuses on Victorian nursemaids and wet nurses. For Hesperus, she has co-authored the Charles Dickens volume in the *Brief Lives* series and co-edited several of Dickens' collaborative Christmas numbers.

HESPERUS PRESS

Hesperus Press, as suggested by the Latin motto, is committed to bringing near what is far – far both in space and time. Works written by the greatest authors, and unjustly neglected or simply little known in the English-speaking world, are made accessible through new translations and a completely fresh editorial approach. Through these classic works, the reader is introduced to the greatest writers from all times and all cultures.

For more information on Hesperus Press, please visit our website:
www.hesperuspress.com

ET REMOTISSIMA PROPE

MODERN VOICES